Curing The Cross-Eyed Mule

Curing The Cross-Eyed Mule

Appalachian Mountain Humor

BY THE EDITORS OF THE BESTSELLING
LAUGHTER IN APPALACHIA

LOYAL JONES AND BILLY EDD WHEELER

August House / *Little Rock*
PUBLISHERS

Published by August House, Inc.,
P. O. Box 3223, Little Rock, Arkansas, 72203,
501-663-7300.

Printed in the United States of America

10 9 8 7 6 5 4 3 2

LIBRARY OF CONGRESS CATALOGING-IN-PUBLICATION DATA

Curing the cross-eyed mule: Appalachian mountain humor / edited by
Loyal Jones and Billy Edd Wheeler.—1st ed.
p. cm.
ISBN 0-87483-083-4 (alk. paper): $8.95
1. Appalachian Region—Social life and customs—Humor.
2. Mountain whites (Southern States)—Humor. 3. American wit and
humor—Appalachian Region. I. Jones, Loyal, 1928-
II. Wheeler, Billy Edd.
PN6231.A65C8 1989
818′ .5402′08975—dc19 88-27317
CIP

Second Printing 1989

Cover illustration by Jan Taylor Weeks
Production artwork by Ira Hocut
Design direction by Ted Parkhurst
Project direction by Hope Norman Coulter

This book is printed on archival-quality paper which meets the
guidelines for performance and durability of the Committee on
Production Guidelines for Book Longevity of the Council on
Library Resources.

AUGUST HOUSE, INC. PUBLISHERS LITTLE ROCK

For anyone on the lookout for a laugh
or other unexpected pleasures

Contents

Preface

Our first book together, *Laughter in Appalachia: A Festival of Southern Mountain Humor,* was so well received that our publishers over at August House asked us to do a second Appalachian humor book. We doubted at first that we could find jokes and stories that were as good as those we had collected over a lifetime and put into the first book, but there was one thing we hadn't counted on. Several readers of the first book couldn't wait to tell us the ones that we hadn't included.

Our greatest satisfaction from the book was that all kinds of people—farmers, tradespeople, laborers, professional people, people in nursing homes, even a man in prison—told us they had enjoyed it and, best of all, sent us stories. We wrote our funny friends all over the place and asked them to send us material, too. In the summer of 1987 we decided to put on another festival of Appalachian humor, which included the following humorists: Anndrena Belcher, Roy Blount, Jr., Manuel "Old Joe" Clark, Jan Davidson, Dr. Carl Hurley, Hannah McConnell, Fred Park, Dr. Tim Stivers, Roni Stoneman, and Dr. William E. Lightfoot. Dr. Michael A. Lofaro contributed a delightful scholarly paper to the festival. We awarded prizes to members of the audience for the best stories in several categories. The festival, held at Berea College, was a huge success, and we have included some of our favorites from that event—contributions from the audience as well as the headliners.

There is no end to stories. They are constantly being generated, or old stories are being recycled to fit new situations. Consider the rash of jokes that followed the discovery that two television evangelists were not as pious as their followers believed. Some of the jokes may have appeared to be sacrilegious, but they were certainly apt social comment. They had a purpose in that they helped people to deal with a bad situation and to realign their thinking about those who claim to be better than the rest of us, and aren't. Because the evangelists' sins were off-color, many of the jokes about them were likewise, so with the good taste we *sometimes* display, we have resisted adding them to the collection. They aren't Appalachian anyway—although as some of the readers of the first book have noted, we have shoe-horned some pretty cosmopolitan or national jokes into our Appalachian format.

Being collectors and basically thieves, we have latched onto anything that tickles us, if by the stretch of our lively imaginations we can see a regional angle. Appalachians are Americans, a part of the great global family, aware of what goes on in the country and the world. We tell stories that reflect more than just life in the region. However, most of the stories included here do depict something of the endlessly intriguing lives of the people of the southern mountains, and most of them are told by natives of the region.

We have tried to credit each source of stories, but we admit that we have long since forgotten where we learned some. In most cases, we have asked permission, but we have lost track of or missed a few of you. Nevertheless, we wanted to include the stories, and we wanted to give you credit for knowing and telling such good stuff. We are grateful to all of you who contributed. We want to thank a few in particular: Judge Sam J. Ervin, III, of the United States Court of Appeals, Fourth Circuit, for permission to use several stories from his late father, Senator Sam J. Ervin, Jr.; Dr. Howard Dorgan, Boone, N.C., who collected and provided Senator Ervin's stories; Jo Lunsford Herrin and the Lunsford family, for permission to use material from their late father, Bascom Lamar Lunsford; Charles Tribble, Cynthiana, Ky.; Dr. Jim Wayne Miller, Bowling Green, Ky.; Charlotte Ross,

Boone, N.C.; Billy Wilson, Berea, Ky.; Paul Graham, Benham, Ky.; Virgil Anderson, Rocky Branch, Ky.; "Old Joe" Clark, Berea, Ky.; Bradley Kincaid, Springfield, O.; James Clifford Terry, Knoxville, Tenn.; and Chet Atkins, C.G.P. (Certified Guitar Player).

We hope you enjoy this book as much as we enjoyed putting it together. We have laughed a lot and felt good in doing so, and we wish the same for you. If you want to tell us some of your stories, we are always ready to drop the other stuff we do and listen.

Billy Edd Wheeler
SWANNANOA, NORTH CAROLINA

Loyal Jones
BEREA, KENTUCKY

Born Modest

LOYAL JONES

One thing I've noticed about growing up in the mountains is that we've had such a load of modesty laid on us, we can't accept a compliment that casts us in a positive light. We don't ever feel right admitting to anything that might make us look proud of doing something right or being a nice person.

I grew up so far back the sun set between our house and the road. We were surely a modest people, but as my father said, we had a whole lot to be modest about. My uncle said that the history of our family could be written on the flyleaf of a pumpkin seed. I've thought about that, and I don't know. It seems to me that we all have about the same amount of history, except that some of us lose it along the way, like pocketknives, tie clips, and that sentimental poetry book Aunt Martha sent us one Christmas. I remember helping this friend from New England move, and I remarked about a bed that had seemed to be around for a good many years.

"Yes," he said. "We come from a long line of people."

"Most of us do," I said.

That is true, whether or not we can name all of our

forebears who walked the earth, toiled, kicked over the traces now and again, dreamed, mourned for something or someone, and reluctantly shuffled off this coil. They were probably as serious about what they were up to as we are, were disappointed in themselves at times, or elated when they overshot their own mark. They humped their loads along, were a part of it all. The writer of Ecclesiasticus could have been talking about them when he wrote, "Some there be, which have no memorial . . . and are become as though they had not been born." He went on to give them a tribute of his own: "Their seed standeth fast and their children for their sakes. Their seeds shall remain forever." The lines remind us to praise not only "famous men"—who get memorialized anyway—but also those who are unremembered. I like to try to imagine those who went before me, the Joneses and Morgans and Holdens and Baties and Bostons and Weathermans, now forgotten, and even before them, those with single common names before surnames were invented. No one in my family knows where any of our forebears landed in this country or where in Wales, Scotland, England, or Germany they lived before they ventured here. Would we recognize them as kindred? Would we like them? How much of what we are did they send down to us in genes and traditions? Plenty, I suspect.

One thing they sent down is a heavy load of Calvinism. It is responsible for most of our humility and modesty and has told us more than we wanted to know about human frailty. I remember this fellow who had a son go to the penitentiary, and he wrote his father, "In here, Daddy, it's just like it is out there. Us Baptists is in the lead." The men's group at the church gave one of my uncles an award for humility, but they took it away when they heard him bragging about it.

We always shied away from praise, as if we thought that if we admitted we were good at something, we'd forget how to do it, or the preacher would make a call on us. So everybody always had some excuse to cover up any talent he had. A neighbor was a good musician, but he had to protest for a while before it seemed right to play. He'd apologize for his banjo's not staying in tune, or for having a cold that made him sound like a bullfrog. This sort of thing went on even if you had just demonstrated that you were good at what it is that you do. If somebody made a fine speech at the Farmer's Federation picnic and was complimented for it, he'd say, "Well, now the reason I was able to do that was that just before I went down there I read this piece in the *Asheville Citizen,* and it gave me the idea. Why, shoot, I'm no speaker." People would say, "Come and go home with us for dinner, if you don't mind poor folks' victuals" (pronounced vittles). Even if somebody complimented one of our children, we'd feel we ought to say, "Well, she does pretty well considering what she's got to work with," or "Yeah, he's right good-looking for a Jones." If someone asked us to help fix something, we'd say, "Well, I'll see what I can do if you don't mind having a jack-leg mechanic tinkering with it." "Oh, that old cake?" my mother would say. "Why I just made that from scratch."

Now why do we do that? Well, why not? If you tell everybody that you are not very good at what you are going to do, you have let yourself off the hook in case you don't do it well. If, on the other hand, you do as well as you think you're going to do anyhow, then everybody is pleasantly surprised. You come out ahead either way. It's good training as a model of modesty for your children. After observing the old folks, they wouldn't dare take credit for something they did. Modesty is a way of life. Somebody asked my grandma if she had seen Halley's Comet in 1910, and she said, "Well, only from a distance."

Lincoln is credited with saying that God must have loved the common people since He made so many of them. He had a good argument, but it is not always obvious who the common people are. On close examination the common people often turn out to be uncommon. Lincoln is the best example most people have heard about, but I find uncommon traits all the time among people who are scarcely noticed by the avowed uncommoners. On the other hand,

the supposed elite often have some pretty common tendencies. I found that out just reading newspaper accounts of the doings of some politicians (I'll not get into the subject of fallen preachers; they seem to deal with each other pretty well). As you know, a dose of school polish will hide a lot but not everything, and a lack of formal schooling doesn't always hinder true wit and talent.

The ordinary country people that I grew up among were a lively and entertaining lot. So far as I can determine they had been on the frontier and in rural areas of this country for six or seven generations, maybe more, since they married young and took seriously the biblical admonition to replenish the earth. They had enjoyed a character-building hard life. They had worked and struggled with destiny, and when they had done all they knew to do, they hunkered down and took what came. But they were not a hard people, as I knew them, but sentimental and loving. We could laugh at ourselves and others, but in a gentle way within the bounds of decorum—and common sense, for our kind of Calvinists were not noted for pacifism.

I believe it was Carlyle who said that a person's religion, or the lack of it, was the most considerable part of him. We were a religious people. Of course the men would sometimes sow a few wild oats in their youth. My father had a few encounters with John Barleycorn, and once in an addled state he wandered into a North Carolina laurel hell where he both froze and sobered through a long winter night. That experience and the influence of my mother, a preacher's daughter, brought him to the Lord, and the church, and a deacon's role. We were Baptists at a time when preachers made frontal assaults on the devil and sin, before social ills and "you're O.K." psychology became popular sermon topics. Even so, we were forgiving and tolerant of human failing—which was good, since there was a right smart of it. Yet much of the time we saw people do what they were expected to do.

The local color writers, when they came down to take a look at us, didn't see the modesty and our cherished tolerance. They saw moonshiners and feudists, and I have to admit that we have liquified a good many bushels of corn and ventilated a few folks, some worthy of the attention. John Fox noticed a connection between white lightning and the proclivity for mayhem. Fox and the other writers were absolutely fascinated by violence, as we all are, and they fed the appetites of supposed gentlefolk in the drawing rooms of the East. In this way, they gave the rest of the world the impression that all we did was swill moonshine and shoot our neighbors. Although some of us do both occasionally, most of us are Bluenoses and are boringly benign.

The missionaries came by the thousands in the first part of this century. In fact, we had more missionaries than any other place on the globe except for Africa, but the difference was that we were already Christian. We were just not the right kind. Calvinism had gone out of fashion in other parts of the country where life had gotten a little easier. Mainstream Christians read the local color novels and the lurid newspaper accounts of the Hatfield-McCoy feud, and the Home Mission Boards decided to send preachers, teachers, and medical people. We thought we already had plenty of preachers, but we were grateful for the teachers and doctors and nurses. We got along pretty well except when our relatives up North sent us one of their fund-raising brochures that let the rest of the world in on our peculiar ways, considerably embellished. But we allowed as how there was a price for everything, especially education. The consolation was that we were a whole lot smarter than they thought, but being modest, we never had the satisfaction of telling them so. Sometimes we played with them. One of the missionaries came by to see an old Baptist fellow and said, "Did you hear that lightning struck the Baptist Church?"

"No," he answered, "I haven't been to that church since they bought that old piano. No doubt the Lord was showing His displeasure about that."

"No, the piano was in the opposite end of the church from the place lightning struck," the missionary said.

"Well," said the old man reflectively, "I guess God hadn't been in that church for so long that He didn't know where that piano was."

Another missionary went to see this woman and asked her if she was lost. "Why, no, I've lived here all of my life," she said.

"It sounds to me as if you're living in darkness," he observed.

"Yeah, that's right. I've been trying to get my husband to cut a new window over on the south side of the house."

"Do you have any Presbyterians around here?"

"I don't think so, but my husband traps all kinds of varmints, and he's got their hides nailed up on the barn. You can go out there and see if he got one of them."

A baby had been crying the whole time, and the visitor thought he'd give some domestic advice since he wasn't getting too far on theological matters. So he observed, "That child is spoiled."

"No," the woman replied. "He always smells that way."

When the warriors in President Johnson's skirmish against poverty came (somebody said they went to Harvard and then turned left to get here), they had their own ideas about us. They did a lot of good, but they too were not content to help us with education, social services, and jobs. They also wanted to change us. They had discovered values, thanks to sociology, and they plotted endlessly for ways to intervene in the cycle of poverty that was the current targetal thrust. We toyed with them too. One well-dressed poverty fighter, driving a fancy car, was asked by a mountain man what he did.

"I'm with the War on Poverty," he said.

"Looks like you won," the mountaineer observed.

The VISTA workers living with mountaineers wrote back

home about all of the things mountain people didn't know about, like museums, subways, and art galleries. Their hosts talked in wonder about people who didn't know how to milk a cow, plant a garden, slaughter a hog, or piece a quilt. Some poverty workers, because our accent was strange to them, thought we didn't understand the English language. One took a course in communicating with the poor, and he came down from Washington to visit some clients with the local worker. They went to see an elderly woman, and the visiting expert kept talking to her in a sort of pidgin English, using one-syllable words, trying to explain his program. When he got up to leave, the lady whispered to the local worker, "That feller's not right bright, is he?"

But you know, a lot of those people who came down to change us have met and married local folks, and not only have they come to like us, they imitate us. For a hundred years now, people have complained about how strange we are, and then they join us! Now they're still saying we are strange, while they take our music and tales, accents, crafts, and dances and make theses and dissertations and books and plays out of them. In the process some of them become our friends for life, move in and wear overalls, CAT hats, and stud-hoss boots, drive pickups. Then they quit talking so much and get modest on us. Give us competition along that line—tear up a banjo, old-time style, and then say, "Shucks, I'm just learning."

When everybody gets in on your act, it ain't no act at all. We may have to start flaunting something or other. Maybe start bragging on our kids. I sure do hate to change, though.

Making Storytelling Seem Unnatural and Other Cultural Observations

ROY BLOUNT, JR.
President of the Foundation of the Singing-Impaired

I never thought of storytelling as an art form. I just thought it was something you did if your mother asked you if you are going to eat your cauliflower, and you said, well, that reminds me of something that happened last week, and you just keep on talking until she forgets about the cauliflower.

I just wonder what the *next* art form will be? I think complaining about your loved ones might be something that people could have festivals on years from now. People sitting around complaining about others. A person could complain about somebody else's mother better than you could complain about your own.

I have spent a good deal of time up in the New York area,

and now live in Massachusetts. I moved up there from Georgia, wanting to be with people who read and talked about books and all. But I got up there and people started talking to me about trucks and how to raise pigs—all kinds of things I didn't even know. When they asked why I didn't know how to fix trucks, I'd just say, "It's not in my line of work."

"What do you do, then?" they'd ask.

"I'm a writer," I say. And they say, "Oh." You know, it's kind of unnatural to say you're a writer. I always feel embarrassed—sort of like saying I'm a desperado or something. When people asked Jesse James what he did, I'm sure he didn't just say, "Rob banks." He'd just probably hem and haw and say, "Something in banks," or something like that.

When I'd tell people I am a writer, a gleam would hit their eye and they'd say, "Oh yeah, you're from the South, so you're a natural storyteller." And that always put me off, 'cause I'd worked at it and all, and didn't see anything natural about it. So what I did over the years was to complicate the thing as much as I could—to make it seem as unnatural as possible.

Translating for Uncle Vernon and the Lady from the East

This is a true story about a 'cultural' thing. A friend of mine down in Tennessee brought a friend home to visit from Connecticut to her parents' home in the hills of Tennessee. The woman from Connecticut was sort of wary about going down there, as she didn't know, you know, if she could get along with people.

My friend assured her that it would be fine, said, "Oh, no, don't worry about it. They'll be friendly. They're nice folks. They'll feed you and take good care of you." Well, she finally agreed she'd go for a short visit.

After they got down there the friend took the Easterner to visit her Uncle Vernon up in the holler, who dipped snuff, and who kept a little streak on his mouth. This lady had never seen anything like that, so she was sort of edging around, and pulled over from Uncle Vernon.

My friend introduced her lady friend to Uncle Vernon and he said, "Well, I'll be. Glad to meet ye. How do you do. And what do you allow?"

The lady from Connecticut said, "I don't allow anything!"

It has to be explained what "allow" meant in the country.

An Essential "Singing-Impaired" Song

I noticed that a lot of the competition here at the Humor Festival is in song. Well, I happen to be the National President of the Foundation of the Singing-Impaired. This is an organization of people who can't sing. You know you are "singing-impaired" if a lot of people are singing in a room and you walk in, and they stop. It happens to us over and over. So the only thing we can do is to just go out and sing anyway, as there are no government programs to help us learn to sing, or to build us a ramp to get us onto the notes, or anything.

I wrote this song. It's an essential singing-impaired song. I sang this one time and someone came up afterwards and said, "Now, that song you just sang—did it just have one note in it?"

That really touched my heart because I'd hoped all along that I had one in there. I'm not sure where it comes in, but if you-all hear it, I would appreciate it if you would raise your hand. It'd make me feel good.

The song goes something like this:

> When you said you were on my side
> You lied
> When you said I'll be satisfied
> You lied
> When you said your love would abide
> You lied
> But when you said you'd hit me
> And knock out my tooth
> You told the truth.

''Something Better Than Squirrel Meat'':

LOVE AND MARRIAGE

It's the Best

My father was courting a girl who loved squirrel meat. One day she asked him to kill her a mess of squirrels. He said that he couldn't because he had to work. She kept after him and finally said, ''If you'll kill me a mess of squirrels I'll give you something better than squirrel.''

So he killed her three nice squirrels, dressed them out, and took them to her. He waited, went to see her several times, but she didn't mention the squirrels and her promise. Finally he said, ''Now, you promised me something better than squirrel if I would kill you a mess of squirrels.''

''Well,'' she said, ''after frying those squirrels and making gravy and eating them with some good biscuits, I've decided that there's nothing better than squirrel.''

Ernie Carpenter
SUTTON, WEST VIRGINIA

Getting Some Wires Crossed

A nice-looking girl from New York City was visiting the hills of West Virginia and had a chance to go to a square dance, where she met a handsome mountain boy. They danced several dances together, and after the dance the boy asked her for her phone number. "It's CApitol 2-8974," she told him.

The boy looked puzzled, paused for a minute, then asked her, "Uh, how do you make a capital 2?"

Billy Edd Wheeler

Bad Geography

A farmboy came to town on Saturday night, went to a bar, and there saw the woman of his dreams. He bought her a drink and asked her to go out with him. "I can't," she said. "I'm a lesbian."

"How's everything in Beirut?" he asked.

Oscar Davidson
SOMERSET, KENTUCKY

Premarital Sects

This man was going with a girl and was wanting to marry her, but she wouldn't even consider it. He kept on pressing her until she finally told him, "Why, Sid, I'm a hermaphrodite."

"Aw," he said, "that's all right, honey. I'll go to your church and you can go to mine. I'm a Campbellite myself."

Curtis Barber
and William E. Lightfoot
BOONE, NORTH CAROLINA

A Helpful Suggestion

The mountain man was doing the best he could to be chivalrous. He carried a washtub on his back and a chicken under his arm, had a cane in one hand and led a calf with the other. Still his new girlfriend was wary. Either that or she was just having some fun. As they approached the dark woods she held back, saying, "I'm afraid to walk with you in there. You might try to hug me and kiss me."

"How on earth do you think I could manage that?" the mountaineer asked. "As you can see, I'm pretty well loaded down."

"Well," she said, "you could stick that cane in the ground, tie the calf up to it, and put the chicken under the washtub."

Billy Edd Wheeler

Thermal Studies

"We all know that the freezing point is 32, but what is the squeezing point?"

"Two in the shade, of course."

James Clifford Terry
KNOXVILLE, TENNESSEE

An Alternative

I was walking around this little town, and I saw one of those signs outside a church that had this message, "If you're through with sin, come on in!" I walked over and looked at it real close, and somebody had taken lipstick and written on the glass, "If you're *not* through, call 854-2234."

Dr. Tim Stivers
LOUISVILLE, KENTUCKY

Country Music Groupies

David Morris's mother has another name for the girls who hang out at bluegrass festivals and chase the musicians. She calls them weed monkeys.

David, West Virginia's great folk singer, asked her how she came up with that name.

"Well," she said, "fellers take 'em out in the weeds and monkey around with 'em."

Billy Edd Wheeler

A Real Skinny Girl

The Big Spender called the bellhop up to his room and announced, "I'd like a woman." The bellhop blushed, said, "I'm sorry, sir, but this is not that kind of a hotel."

"Are you sure?" the man said, peeling off a hundred-dollar bill and handing it to the bellhop, who stared at the bill, gulped, and said, "Well . . . what kind of woman did you want?"

"She has to be at least six-foot-three and weigh not over a hundred and ten pounds," Big Spender said, to which the bellhop allowed there was no such woman in town. "Are you sure?" Big Spender asked, peeling off another hundred-dollar bill.

"If there is, I'll find her," the bellhop affirmed, leaving the room quickly, two hundred dollars richer. Soon he was back with a woman six feet six inches tall, weighing ninety-eight pounds. She was so thin she could hide behind a rope. She'd have to stand twice to cast a shadow. The man looked at her and declared she would do. "Take off your clothes," he said.

The lady huffed, "Humphht, I'm not that kind of girl!"

"Are you sure?" Big Spender said, peeling off a hundred-dollar bill and handing it to her. She took off her clothes. He studied her, said, "You're perfect. Now, get down on your hands and knees."

"I ain't about to do that," the girl said, in no uncertain terms, and Big Spender said, "Are you sure?" He peeled off another hundred from his huge bankroll. The lady dropped suspiciously to her hands and knees as the man walked around her, surveying her critically. Then he walked to the closet, opened the door, and out sprang a big skinny English bird dog.

The man pointed at the girl while addressing the dog sternly. "Now you look at her," he said. "Take a good look, cause that's what you're gonna look like if you don't start eating your Gravy Train!"

Billy Edd Wheeler

Snuffy and the Law

When Snuffy Jenkins was a young man, he was parked in a car with this girl one night, and a deputy sheriff came up with a flashlight, shined it in his face, and asked, "What are you doing?"

"Nothing."

"What have you been doing?"

"Nothing."

"What are you going to do?"

"Nothing."

"Well, you hold the light and let me get in there."

Homer "Pappy" Sherrill
CHAPIN, SOUTH CAROLINA

Distraction

When Sam saw Joe one morning, Joe looked terrible. "What's the matter, Joe?"

"I didn't sleep a wink last night."

"Why?"

"The shades were up all night."

"Well, why didn't you pull them down?"

"I couldn't reach all the way across the street."

Loyal Jones

Even the Pipes Were Sexy

I got into a little plumbing job at my house, and I noticed that I had two different sizes of pipe to connect, so I sent my son Gregg down to the hardware store to get an adapter. A few minutes later he came rolling back into the driveway, and he didn't have it, so I asked why not.

"When I asked for the adapter, the clerk wanted to know if I wanted a male or a female adapter."

"Well, what'd you tell him?" I asked.

"I told him that all we wanted to do was fix the kitchen sink and that we didn't want to raise any little ones."

So I said let's go back down there and get this straightened out. When we got to the hardware store, the clerk he had talked to was out to lunch and there was this girl there. She asked if she could help and I said, "Yes, I need a female three-quarter-to-one-half-inch adapter."

Well, she looked kind of puzzled, but she went back and looked on the shelves and through a catalogue and then she came back and said, "Sir, I think for what you need you'll have to go over to the drugstore."

Richard Collins
HUNTINGTON, WEST VIRGINIA

Kissing Kin

It was called a Full Moon Bluegrass Pickin' Party and it was in high gear, with the music going at its foot-stomping best, the moon shining bright, and the moonshine flowing free. One banjo picker, taking a break to have another drink, was feeling kind of amorous. He spotted a shapely girl standing all alone in the moonlight by a tree, so he slipped up behind her, grabbed her, and kissed her.

"How dare you!" she said, as she spun around and slapped his face.

He was quick to apologize. "I'm sorry, lady, I beg your pardon. I thought you was my sister."

"You danged fool," she yelled, "I *am* your sister!"

Billy Edd Wheeler

He Said It Wasn't His

Dewitt (pronounced Dee-witt) Deweese was hauled into court on a paternity suit by the girl he'd been dating some. Before she had the baby she went down to where he worked and caught him on his lunch break. She pulled back her coat and showed him that she was pregnant. "Look what you done to me," she said, pointing to her large belly. "What I want to know is what you're going to do about it?"

"I did that?" Dewitt said.

"Yes, you most certainly did."

"Well, uh, 'scuse me," Dewitt said, and he thought that was the end of it. Until he received the summons.

After the judge heard the case he declared that he believed Dewitt was father of the child and ordered him to pay child support.

"But Judge, Your Honor," Dewitt protested. "Look at that baby and then look at me. That baby don't look nothing like me!"

"You feed him till he does," the judge said.

Chet Atkins
NASHVILLE, TENNESSEE

Gentlemen

A traveling salesman was overtaken by night along a lonely road, and he made his way to a farmer's house. "May I spend the night here?" he asked.

"Yes," said the farmer, "if you don't mind sleeping with that red-headed schoolteacher who boards here."

"That's fine," said the salesman. "I am a gentleman."

"Good," said the farmer. "So is he."

Loyal Jones

Clumsy

Two farmers talking: "What happened to the wheel on your wagon?"

"The hired hand busted it on a rock."

"Is that the same hired hand who got your daughter in trouble?"

"Yep."

"Clumsy, ain't he?"

Fred Domville
PRAIRIE VILLAGE, KANSAS

The Stubborn Fiancé

A bunch of fellows from Evarts, Kentucky, got to talking about one of their friends who had just got engaged to a young woman who had a bad reputation. But she was the first sweetheart this fellow had ever had, and he was just crazy about her. These guys thought that he ought to be told about her reputation. He was an innocent sort of fellow, and it didn't seem right for him to marry the woman without being told about her. So they decided that this big football player would go tell him—figured he wouldn't hit *him.* So the football player found him and said, "Look, you can't marry Sue Ellen. She's slept with ever man in Evarts."

The fellow looked pained and said, "Well, Evarts ain't no real big place."

Dr. Charles L. Cox
OAK RIDGE, TENNESSEE

Getting Married

My mother always said I ought to remember the day I was born, but I never could. I like to've never got married on account of that. My wife wouldn't have me. I tried to tell her my life's history, but she wouldn't pay no attention to me, so I just had to steal her. She wouldn't have me atall. I was bashful then and didn't hardly know what to say. I left her standing out there outside the courthouse, and I said, "There's a good-looking girl out there that wants to get married."

"Well," they said. "I guess you want a license."

"Yeah."

They said I'd have to prove that I was eighteen, and her too. I said I wasn't there when she was born, so I couldn't swear to her age, or mine either. I said I couldn't remember the day I was born. I've tried my best to remember, but I can't. They said that if I could prove I was born and raised, they'd give us a license. I nearly ran myself to death trying to find out whether I'd been born or not. People said, "Well, we don't know whether or not you have been born. For all we know the crows may have laid you on a stump and the sun hatched you. We don't know for certain." They said, "You may have been born, but you don't look like nothing that has been raised." I never had such a time in my life trying to get my license. Mabel was standing out there in the hot sun looking like the Statue of Liberty. I finally ran into a fellow who said, "There's a blacksmith shop down there. See him."

I went down there, and he said, "Yeah." He hammered me out a license there, and I've been with her sixty years. That's why there are so many separations these days. The licenses wear out. They don't mean to separate; but their licenses wear out. Paper soon rots out. You get a blacksmith that knows his business to hammer you out a license, and you've got something that will stay with you.

Virgil Anderson
ROCKY BRANCH, KENTUCKY

Starting Early

James Still of Hindman, Kentucky, told me this story. He said he heard it at a church association meeting in Alabama that he attended with his father when he was a boy. An old man there took a gold watch out of his pocket, opened it, and ceremoniously announced that at that very moment, fifty-five years before, he was married. Then he told an anecdote about the wedding night which he and his bride had spent in her home. They were arranged to sleep in a big four-poster bed that had rather low, sharp points on the posts. The groom blew out the lamp and started to bed. Being in a strange place, he stumbled in the dark, fell forward, and hit himself in the eye on one of the sharp bedposts. The next morning he discovered he had a black eye, and when they went to the breakfast table his father-in-law took one look at him and said, "Fighting already!"

Dr. Jim Wayne Miller
BOWLING GREEN, KENTUCKY

Research

A little town had a high birth rate that had attracted the attention of the sociologists at the state university. They wrote a grant proposal, got a huge chunk of money, hired a few additional sociologists, an anthropologist, a family planning and birth control specialist, moved to town, rented offices, set up their computers, got squared away, and began designing their questionnaires and such. While the staff was busy getting ready for their big research effort, the project director decided to go to the local drugstore for a cup of coffee. He sat down at the counter, ordered his coffee, and while he was drinking it, he told the druggist what his purpose was in town, then asked him if he had any idea why the birthrate was so high. ''Sure,'' said the druggist. ''Every morning the six o'clock train comes through here and blows for the crossing. It wakes everybody up, and, well, it's too late to go back to sleep, and it's too early to get up.''

Loyal Jones

Thinking It Over

A man with fourteen children made a promise that if he and his wife had one more, he's go out and hang himself. Within the year, she delivered up a fifteenth child. He got a rope and went out into the woods. After a while he came back and explained, ''I got to looking at that rope over the limb, and then I got to thinking that I might be hanging an innocent man.''

Bob Sears
SOMERSET, KENTUCKY

No Time for Music

There were twenty-three of us children, full-blooded brothers and sisters. There was this French lady, a Catholic, who used to come by our house from time to time. This lady was concerned about my mother's health because she had so many young'ns. I was the seventeenth child, by the way.

''Mrs. Stoneman,'' she asked one day, ''have you ever heard of the rhythm method?''

Now, all of us picked an instrument and Mom was so used to musicians around the house, she said, ''Well, who would want to get a band together at three o'clock in the morning!''

Roni Stoneman
NASHVILLE, TENNESSEE

A Costly Hearing Problem

I was the seventeenth child of twenty-three children. The reason there were so many of us was my mother was hard of hearing. That is true. Daddy would say at bedtime every

night to Mama, "You want to go to sleep or what?"
Mama would say, "What?"

Roni Stoneman

The Lawyer Couple and the Live-In Maid

A county seat lawyer and his wife advertised for a live-in maid to cook and do the housework. A likely-looking girl came in from the country, and they hired her. She worked out fine, was a good cook, was polite, and kept the house neat. One day, after about six months, she came in and said she would have to quit. "But why?" asked the disappointed wife. She hemmed and hawed and said she didn't want to say, but the wife was persistent, and so she said, "Well, on my day off a couple of months ago I met this good-looking fellow from over in the next county, and well—I'm pregnant." The woman said, "Look, we don't want to lose you. My husband and I don't have any children, and we'll adopt your baby if you will stay." She talked to her husband, he agreed, and the maid said she would stay. The baby came, they adopted it, and all went well.

After several months, though, she came again and said that she would have to quit. So the wife questioned her, found that she was pregnant again, talked to her husband, and offered to adopt the baby if she would stay. She agreed, had the baby, they adopted it, and life went on as usual.

In another few months, however, she again said she would have to leave. Same thing. She was pregnant. They made the same offer, she agreed, and they adopted the third baby. She worked for week or two, but then said, "I am definitely leaving this time."

"Don't tell me you are pregnant again?" asked the lady of the house.

"No," she said, "there are just too many kids here to pick up after."

Loyal Jones

The Hammock in the Attic

A man came tiptoeing in with his shoes in his hand one morning about 5:30, after an all-night poker game, and as he passed his wife's bed she looked up at him and said, in her gruffest voice, "George, what are you doing coming in at this time of the night?"

He thought she was asleep, so it surprised him so much he had a hard time thinking up an excuse. He stuttered around, hemming and hawing, and finally told her, "Uh, honey, I got in so late last night I decided the best thing to do was not to wake you up, so I slept in the hammock on the porch. Then the birds got to chirping, woke me up, so I figured I'd just come on up."

"George," she said, even gruffer than before, "I took the hammock down two weeks ago and put it in the attic."

Poor George was really addled now. He dropped his shoes, faced her, and said in his bravest voice, "Well, that's my story, and I'm sticking to it!"

Billy Edd Wheeler

He Doesn't Make Sense

This woman went to see a lawyer about getting a divorce. The lawyer started to ask her some routine questions. "What are your grounds?"

"Well, we have this great big farm."

"Do you have some sort of grudge?"

"No, he's never built one, and we have to park outside."

"Well, does he beat you up?"

"Are you kidding? I get up two hours before he does."

"Look, lady, why do you want to divorce him?"

"Because I can never carry on an intelligent conversation with that man."

Loyal Jones

A Very Reverent Golfer

Fred and Bill were having their weekly round of golf at the Land o' Sky Golf Course and as they were walking down the fairway on the long par-five number six hole a funeral procession drove by them along River Road. Fred took off his golf hat, held it over his heart and stood motionless, watching the cars drive slowly by with their lights on.

Bill was touched. He didn't know Fred was so religious, or sensitive, walked up to him and said, "That was a nice thing to do, Fred. Was that somebody you knew that died?"

"Yes," Fred said, wiping away a tear as he pulled a four-wood from his bag, "she was my wife. We'd a-been married twenty-eight years today, if she'd lived."

Billy Edd Wheeler

Coincidence

There was a man who took this woman to court and accused her of assault and battery. The judge asked him what she did to him.

"She hit me and beat me in the face," he said.

So the judge asked the woman why she had hit him. "He called me a two-bit prostitute."

"What did you hit him with?" asked the judge.

"A sack full of quarters."

Billy Wilson
BEREA, KENTUCKY

Ugly

He was like myself, a big ugly sort of fellow. He wasn't broke out with good looks.

Virgil Anderson
ROCKY BRANCH, KENTUCKY

The Mirror

This farming couple had lived a very primitive life in the backwoods without modern conveniences. On his semi-annual trip to town for staples, the farmer went into a store and saw a mirror for the first time. He held it up, saw himself and exclaimed, "Why, that's a picture of my daddy." He bought the mirror, but because his wife had never liked his father, he hid the mirror in his barn and would go out periodically to stare at it.

His wife got suspicious of his extra trips to the barn, and

one day she followed him and watched him looking at the mirror. After he had gone back to the house, she got the mirror out, held it up, and said, "So this-here's that hussy he's been running around with!"

Paul Nestor
LEXINGTON, KENTUCKY

Now, the Strawberries

A farmer was selling strawberries door to door in Asheville, and he went up to a nice house and knocked on the door. A pretty woman came to the door, and he asked her if she would like to buy some strawberries. "Come around to the back door," she said. So he went around to the back door, and the woman opened it and was standing there with nothing on.

The man began to sniffle and then to sob.

"Why, what on earth is the matter?" she asked.

"Well," he said. "It's been a hard year. My mule died, and I didn't hardly raise any crops. My barn burned down, my cow went dry, my wife ran off with a fertilizer salesman, and now I can see that I'm about to be snookered out of my strawberries!"

Dr. Cratis D. Williams
BOONE, NORTH CAROLINA

Lucky Winner

"The man who married Ethel got a prize."

"What was it?"

James Clifford Terry
KNOXVILLE, TENNESSEE

Uh-Oh

A woman got off a bus in a small town with a breast hanging out of her dress. A conscientious policeman rushed up and said, "You are under arrest."

"Why?" she asked, and he pointed at her breast.

"Oh, my gosh," she said. "I forgot the baby!"

Chad Spring
BEREA, KENTUCKY

The Wife and the Mistress

Two men were having an awfully slow round of golf because the two ladies in front of them managed to get into every sand trap, lake, and rough on the course, and they didn't bother to wave the men on through, which is proper golf etiquette.

After two hours of waiting and waiting one man said, "I think I'll walk up there and ask those gals to let us play through." He walked out the fairway, got halfway to the ladies, stopped, turned around, and came back, explaining, "I can't do it. One of those women is my wife and the other is my mistress. Maybe you'd better go talk to them."

The man walked toward the ladies, got halfway there, and, just as his partner had done, stopped, turned around and walked back.

He smiled sheepishly and said, "Small world."

Billy Edd Wheeler

Free Sex with Fill-Up

Two Raleigh County boys were driving through Madison, West Virginia, which is the county seat of Boone County, and one of them noticed a sign at a filling station that said "Free Sex With Fill-up."

"Did you see that?" the one on the passenger side said to the driver.

"Yeah, I did, but I figure it's some kind of scam," the driver said.

"Why don't we give it a shot?"

The driver shrugged and turned around, pulled into the filling station, filled up, paid and waited. When the attendant didn't say anything, he said, "Hey, what about the free sex with the fill-up?"

"Oh, yeah," the attendant said absentmindedly. "Well, you have to guess a number between one and ten."

"Six," the driver said.

"Sorry, it was seven," the attendant said, and walked back inside.

As they drove away the driver said, "See, I told you it

was a scam. Ain't nothing to it but a gimmick. We've been had."

"Naw, now, it's for real," the passenger said. "I know, cause my wife's been here twice for a fill-up, and she guessed the right number both times."

Billy Edd Wheeler

Golden Opportunity

Judge: "Before I pass sentence, tell me, what made you strike your wife?"

Hillbilly: "Well, sir, she had her back to me—she was bent over—the frying pan was handy—and the back door was open. So I just thought I'd take a chance."

Billy Edd Wheeler

The Husband Shopping

Customer (walking into the store past the proprietor): "I just came in to see if I could get something for my wife."

Proprietor: "Well, how much you want for her?"

Billy Edd Wheeler

Good Pay

A man was out mowing his lawn one day, doing a real good job. A fancy-dressed woman came by, driving a big car, stopped, complimented him on his work, and then asked, "How much do you get for mowing a lawn?"

"I get to sleep with the lady of the house," he replied.

Dave Craig
MT. VERNON, KENTUCKY

Qualified

A man had four sons but he had only one toy for them. So he said, "I'm going to give this to the one has never talked back to your mother and has always done what he was told to do."

The boys looked at one another, and then one said, "Dad, I guess you're going to get to play with it."

Bud Lane
MT. STERLING, KENTUCKY

Too Discriminating

A man's wife got to complaining and one day she hit him. He said, "What was that for?"

She said, "Poor bed partner!"

He studied on that for a few days, and then he hit her. She said, "What was that for?"

He said, "For knowing the difference!"

Glenn Baker
FAIRMONT, WEST VIRGINIA

About Even

Husband: "Why are you so beautiful and yet so stupid?"

Wife: "I have to be beautiful so you'll love me, and I have to be stupid so *I* can love *you*."

Loyal Jones

Practice Makes Perfect

A little boy had been studying music in school, and he couldn't wait to share his new knowledge with his parents and visiting dinner guests. "Johann Sebastian Bach had fourteen children, and he practiced on the spinster in his attic!"

Loyal Jones

Might As Well

This is the only joke I ever heard my daddy tell—Bryan Wilson was his name. He'd tell this about the man that would run around, drink and gamble, come in late at night, and then he'd catch the devil from his wife. She harped at him for months, and it wasn't doing a bit of good. She was telling her next-door neighbor about it, and she said, "Why don't you try a little psychology on him? You can catch more flies with sugar than vinegar."

She said, "Well, I'll try anything."

That night when her husband came in late, she said, "Come on in, honey." He looked at her kind of funny and came on in.

"Have this nice chair here," she said, and he looked

funny at her again and sat down. She said, "I'll go fix you something to eat." She went in and fixed him a snack. In a little while she said, "Honey, let's go in the bedroom."

He said, "Might as well. I'll catch the devil when I get home anyway."

Billy Wilson
BEREA, KENTUCKY

Once Was Enough

This man lived in a neighborhood, and when a new neighbor moved in, he tried to be nice to him. He was talking across the fence and said, "How's about you and me going bowling this afternoon?"

The new neighbor said, "I tried that once and didn't like it."

So a couple of days later he thought he'd ask him if he wanted to go fishing. The newcomer said, "No, I tried that once and didn't like it."

A few days later he said to himself, "I'll try one more time." He said, "How about you and me going to play golf?"

"I tried that once and didn't like it." About that time a car pulled up, and the newcomer said, "There comes my son."

He said, "No doubt your *only* son."

Billy Wilson
BEREA, KENTUCKY

Sweet Talk

"Whenever my wife wants some money, she calls me handsome."

"Handsome?"

"Yes, hand some over."

James Clifford Terry
KNOXVILLE, TENNESSEE

A Man of Few Words

A rough-looking but mild-mannered mountain man married a town girl who was known to be outspoken and naggy. But she was a pretty thing, decked out in her white wedding dress, and the mountaineer was mighty proud as he helped her up on his finest mule and led them back into the hills.

Once, going up a steep and rocky path, the mule stumbled, then stopped in its tracks and refused to take another step. The man walked back, looked the mule in the eyes, said, "That's once," and led the mule onward. Pretty soon the mule stumbled again, and stopped. Wouldn't budge, no matter how hard the man pulled at the rope halter. So he walked back, looked the mule in the eyes, said quietly but sternly, "That's twice."

The third time the mule balked, the mountain man walked back, pulled his pistol, and shot the mule dead. He picked up his bride's bag and walked on up the hill, with her following behind on foot, furious at him. She fumed, "Now look what you've done, you ignorant, heartless hillbilly! You're thoughtless and cruel. My feet ache, my dress is a mess. I never should've married an inhumane brute like you. See if I cook you any supper!"

She gave him a real tongue-lashing. Then he walked back to her and said, "That's once."

Billy Edd Wheeler

Upset

A man came to work every day voicing his suspicions that his wife was seeing another man. One morning he rushed in and shouted, "I was right! I came home from work last night and caught her with another man!"

"Well, what did you do?" his friends asked.

"It made me so mad I wouldn't eat a bite of supper, and very little for breakfast!"

John Burgett
BEREA, KENTUCKY

Likely Suspect

A man knocked on the door of a mental institution and asked to see the doctor in charge. "Have any of your male inmates escaped recently?" he asked.

"No," answered the doctor. "Why?"

"Because somebody has run off with my wife," he explained.

Loyal Jones

Sounds Reasonable

A man came home early from work one afternoon and found his wife in the living room with a naked man. "Dear, this is a nudist who came in to use the phone," she explained.

Thomas Chapman
BEREA, KENTUCKY

Blind Assessment

"What do you think of Bill's new wife?"

"Well, I could-a shut my eyes and re'ched out and got something better."

Melvin Higgins
BEREA, KENTUCKY

New Prospects

Hubert had been unfaithful to his wife, and his conscience was getting the better of him, so he told his best friend, "I'm going to confess, and I believe she will forgive me." He went home and told his wife of his infidelity. She immediately asked with whom he had been unfaithful, but he said he couldn't tell her that.

"Was it Myrtle Green?"

"No."

"Was it Mabel Johnson?"

"No."

"Well, was it Ruby Nell Yocum then?"

"No."

"If you don't tell me who it was, I'll not forgive you," she said.

The next day Hubert saw his friend. "Did your wife forgive you?" he asked.

"No," said Hubert, "but she gave me three good leads."

Loyal Jones

Mule Shortage

Every Saturday a farmer and his wife came to the country store to buy groceries. He rode a mule, and she walked behind him carrying the groceries. One day the storekeeper asked him, "Wouldn't it be better if your wife could ride too?"

"Yep," the farmer replied, "but she ain't got no mule."

Calvin Phipps
HENDERSONVILLE, NORTH CAROLINA

The Result of No Vices

A ragged bum stopped a well-dressed man on the streets of Charleston, West Virginia, and hit him up for food money.

"I'll do better than that," the well-dressed man said, figuring the bum really wanted the money for wine or whiskey, anyway. "Come into the bar with me and I'll buy you a drink."

"Thanks, but no thanks," the bum replied, "I'm not a drinking man."

"Well, then, have a smoke on me," he said, pulling out a pack of cigarettes.

"No, thanks, I don't smoke."

The well-dressed man was determined. "Okay," he said, "let's go out to the race track and I'll place a bet for you on a horse that's a shoo-in to win. You can take your winnings and buy new clothes, lots of food, whatever it is that you want."

"Please, sir," the bum said, "I don't need all that. I don't want all that. I only want enough for a small meal."

"In that case, how'd you like to come home and have dinner with me? In fact, I would consider it a favor if you would. I'd like my wife to see for herself what happens to a guy who doesn't smoke, drink, or gamble."

Billy Edd Wheeler

A Resemblance

"Somebody said your wife looks just like Monroe."

"That's right."

"Really?"
"Yes."
"Marilyn?"
"No, Bill."

"Old Joe" Clark
BEREA, KENTUCKY

The Widow and the Eulogy

A woman lost her husband in the flu epidemic of 1918, and undertakers were busy, ministers were busy, doctors and nurses were busy, everybody was busy. But finally she and her children went to the funeral with the proper arrangements. The minister began his discourse. He talked about what a good father the deceased had been, what a good provider he was, how well he was thought of by the people he dealt with and the people he'd worked with. He spoke of how good he had been to his family and his church and so on. He was very complimentary about this unfortunate man. The widow, seated up pretty close to the casket, bent over and spoke to her little son, says, "You look over there, honey, and see if that really is your paw."

Bascom Lamar Lunsford
LEICESTER, NORTH CAROLINA

A Song That Came Out of Two Stories

I was playing golf at a resort town near Asheville, North Carolina, and in my foursome was a man I'd heard was pretty rich. Or at least he'd married money, which I figured was all the same.

Let's call him Selby Winthrop. When I saw him he was the picture of sophistication and affluence—nice golf togs, silvery hair on the sides, and a voice that was cultured and gentlemanly. I was almost intimidated by his Royal Richness, but I decided that I would not be on the defensive, I would wait and see what kind of man he was, try not to be prejudiced against him just because he was rich.

Turned out he was a really nice guy, and with golf, you know, being the great leveler of society that it is, pretty soon we were talking and joking like old friends. I hadn't asked him about his wealth, but soon, after hooking two shots deep into the woods, then dropping a ball and chilly-dipping it down the fairway about fifty yards—a shot we call a "worm-burner"—Mr. Winthrop blushed in embarrassment, turned to me, and said, "I guess you heard that I married into money."

"Yes, sir," I replied. "I think that's grand."

He winked, shook his head, smiled a candid smile that had some sadness in it, leaned close and spoke to me in a tone of confidence. He said, "Billy, let me tell you something. Anytime you marry for money—you *earn* every damn penny of it!"

The uncle of my friend, Skinny McKinney, was a gregarious old gent, and the night I met him he was playing the grand host, buying everybody drinks at the bar (he'd had several himself, his nose lit up like Rudolph the Rednosed Redneck), slapping Skinny's friends on the back, cracking jokes and making merry smalltalk. I'd just met him myself but he'd slapped my back several times too, already.

Uncle McKinney was dressed—actually he was overdressed for that hot summer night—like a mountaineer playboy. Had on a suit, a straight business suit, a silver tie (like gangsters wear in the old movies), wingtip shoes, had his hair slicked back with a fragrant hair dressing, rings flashing on both fingers, and a gold stretch watchband that showed when his cufflinked shirt slid up on his arm. Beads of sweat glistened on his forehead, but he was having a good time.

"What's the occasion?" I asked Skinny.

"He's celebrating his last divorce," he told me. "I think it's his third one. He's a character, ain't he? Drink up, Songwriter, he's buying. Have some shrimp cocktail. You know they fly this stuff in here fresh from New York or someplace twice a week!"

Skinny was not the one to pass up free food or drink, but I was tired and wanted to get back to bed. He'd called me, woken me up, said I had to get dressed and come meet his uncle. Said I might want to write a song about him. I was beginning to think I'd made a mistake and was looking for a polite way to skip out when Uncle McKinney put his arm around me, leaned his red nose down in close proximity to mine, said, "Billy Edd, my last wife was half bulldog and half Indian." He laughed a loud whiskey laugh.

"How's that?" I said.

"Well, she was either on the warpath or sitting around on her ass-end a-growling."

I expected another big laugh, but the twinkle in his eye faded somewhat. He'd made a point by coining a phrase. I didn't know if he made it up or was quoting somebody. I didn't know if he was serious or only half serious, because the twinkle didn't disappear completely, but I did know as soon as I heard it that I was glad I'd stayed long enough to hear it. My butterfly net snatched it out of the alcoholic air and I pinned it to that wall in my mind where rare specimens go to rest, waiting to be used.

"My last wife was half bulldog and half Indian" was pinned beside the phrase "If you marry for money you earn every damned penny of it," and I knew at once that I had a place for both of them. The next day I wrote the song, and here is how it came out:

Gimme Back My Blues

Way down in southern West Virginia
Lived a girl they called Imogene
Her old man died and left her his money
He was a coalfield king
Imogene told me: "If you'll be my husband
I'll dress you in patent leather shoes"
Well, hello good times, so long rambling
Bye-bye down-and-out blues

Chorus
My mama she told me don't marry for money
She may act just like a queen

She may be rich, but there's always a hitch
They can talk sweet and still be mean
Now, buddy, I know, don't you marry for dough
I remember when I didn't have any
I'm telling you, son, if you marry for money
You're gonna earn every penny

Well, Imogene she never took her hair down
She just loafed around dressed in her slip
I couldn't drink beer or smoke my cigars
She was so good at cracking that whip
She was half Indian and half bulldog
That's why I'm a coyote howling
She's either on the warpath or laying round the house
Sitting on her tail end a-growling

Chorus

Now, breakfast in bed ain't too bad for your head
If you're laying there enjoying the snack
But it ain't so much fun if you're the one carrying
And she's propped up in the sack
My mama she told me, "Don't marry for money
You're better off with holes in your shoes"
So I'm gonna run, being rich ain't no fun
Hey, Judge, gimme back my blues!

Billy Edd Wheeler

At Last

Three men were talking about when life begins. The first said he believed it begins at conception. The second thought it begins at birth. The third one said, "You're wrong. It begins when the kids leave home and the dog dies."

Dr. Robert Johnstone
BEREA, KENTUCKY

REPORT CARD
D+

''Knowing What Ain't So'':

SCHOOLS AND EDUCATION

Preference

Josh Billings said, ''It is better to be ignorant than to know what ain't so.''

Sen. Sam J. Ervin, Jr.
MORGANTON, NORTH CAROLINA

Grade School Gambler

One little tow-headed mountain boy about ten years old was known to gamble on anything. If two birds sat on a wire, he'd bet on which one would fly first, or which water streak would go down the window quickest in a rain, anything. And he won most of the time.

One day he stopped his teacher in the hall as she was rushing toward the classroom, said, ''Miss Grundy, I bet you five dollars you've got on pink panties today.''

It was awfully brash for a boy of ten and the teacher didn't like it a bit. She almost sent him to the principal's office, but she thought she'd just teach him a lesson. So she quickly retorted, ''Okay, I'll take that bet!''

She led him aside and pulled her skirt part-way up her hip and let him see the lower edge of her panties, which were blue. The boy gave her five dollars. She called his father and said, "Well, sir, I think I've probably cured your son of gambling." And she told him what happened.

"Why, that little skunk!" the father said. "He bet me ten dollars this morning that before the day was over he'd get you to show him your underwear!"

Billy Edd Wheeler

Checking Her Over

A kindergarten class went on a field trip to the stockyards. They saw the men moving the cattle around in the pens and in the show ring. When they got back to school, the teacher asked them if they had any questions about what they had seen. One little boy said, "Yeah, why do those men slap those cows on the rear end?" The teacher knew a little about cows, but not much, and she explained that this was the way they decided whether or not these were good cows. She said, "If you're going to buy a cow, you slap her on the rear end."

That satisfied him, but a little while later, she sent that same boy to the lunchroom to find out what they were going to serve for lunch. The boy came back and said, "We're going to have hamburger and french fries and milk and beans, and, oh yeah, the principal's up there, and I think he's going to buy one of the cooks."

Charles Tribble
CYNTHIANA, KENTUCKY

Not I

This little boy named Johnny was bad to lay out of school and say that he had been sick. One day when he did not show up for school, the principal called his house. He heard a small voice and asked why Johnny wasn't in school. "Oh, he's bad sick today. Too sick to go to school," the voice said.

"With whom am I speaking?" the principal asked.

"My brother," said the voice.

Rev. Gifford Walters
MONTICELLO, KENTUCKY

Body Parts

A little boy came home from school one day and announced that he had learned two parts of the body that he's never heard of before. "What are they?" asked his father."

"Vestibule and rotunda," answered the little boy.

"Those are not body parts. Why do you think they are?" "Well, we were studying about this politician that got shot, and the book said he was shot once in the vestibule and twice in the rotunda."

June Rice
PAINTSVILLE, KENTUCKY

Just Trying To Be Helpful

A little boy came back from a program down at the school with two black eyes. His mother asked what happened. "Well, this woman in front of me stood up, and she had her dress caught in her crack, so I pulled it out. She got mad and hit me in my right eye."

"What happened to your left eye?" she asked.

"That's when I decided that she wanted it back where it was."

Loyal Jones

And the Teacher Have Give Up

This little boy had a hard time with his grammar. His main problem was with past participles. One day he wrote a theme, handed it in, and said, "I have wrote you a good one this time, teacher." The teacher thought this was a good time to teach him a lesson, so she directed him to stay after school and write "I have written" two hundred times. She left him with his work, and the next morning when she came to school, she found a note from the boy, "Dear Teacher, I have wrote the assignment 200 times and now I have went home."

Loyal Jones

Too Dangerous

This man met his son's teacher in town one day and he asked how his son was doing in school.

"Oh, he's doing real well, but you ought to get him an encyclopedia."

"He'd break his fool neck. He'd never learn to ride it," said the father.

Max Woody
OLD FORT, NORTH CAROLINA

Stick to Your Job

A teacher in a country school had a boy in class who was very dirty and smelly, so she wrote a note for him to take home to his mother: "Your son smells bad. Please give him a bath."

The next day the boy came with a note from his mother: "Your job is to learn him, not smell him."

Dr. Oscar Gunkler
BEREA, KENTUCKY

Name Calling

Edith Waites, who taught fifth grade at Connorsville School, used to tell the story about getting a phone call one night from a woman who wanted to know just what she was teaching her son. She said, "He's in there working his arithmetic, and he's saying, 'Twenty-seven and forty-two, the son of a bitch is sixty-nine. Nine and twelve, the son of a bitch is twenty-one.' Now, I just want to know what you're telling him to make him talk like that."

Well, it sort of floored Mrs. Waites for a while, but then she got to thinking about what she had said, and she remembered that she had told them that day when they were working their arithmetic to say, "the sum of which" in giving the answer.

Charles Tribble
CYNTHIANA, KENTUCKY

Boy with a Lamp

I couldn't remember who that man was in mythology who went around with a lamp looking for an honest man. So I asked my literary advisers, Ed and Polly Cheek, and they told me it was Diogenes.

When I was a student down at Chapel Hill, I met a fellow who had just moved there to retire. Seems like about every day he would be over in the library checking out a great big stack of books. One day he was talking about how students don't seem to read much these days or know much of anything, and he told me this story:

A boy came down out of the mountains one time to attend school there at Chapel Hill, and he was moving from one place to another and had some things in his hands, including a lamp, and so my friend saw him and said, "Hello, is your name Diogenes?"

"No," the boy said, "it's Johnson."

Loyal Jones

But He Knows His History

Son to father: "Here's my report card and one of yours I found in the attic."

Dr. Charles S. Webster
NAPLES, FLORIDA

He's Not Bad in Science Either

Son to father: "Here is my report card. What do you think—heredity or environment?"

Dr. Charles S. Webster

The Dreadful C

Dad: "Where's your report card?"

Son: "It drowned."

Dad: "How's that?"
Son: "It's all below C-level."

Dr. Dorothy Gates
ST. PETERSBURG, FLORIDA

Close

"I hear your boy won a prize in school?"

"Yep, he did, and I'm proud of him."

"What did he do?"

"Well, the teacher asked how many legs a dog has. He said three, and that was the closest to the right answer."

Loyal Jones

Say What?

In the earlier days the Hindman Settlement School at the Forks of Troublesome Creek could accommodate only one hundred "scholars" and had an excess of several hundred applicants to choose from. The directors were careful to select the most apt and the most deserving. They required an interview with a parent before the final decision to enroll a child, and that the child be innoculated for typhoid fever as there were occasional outbreaks of the disease in the county. One day the lady director while interviewing the father of a prospective student inquired if his son had been innoculated. The father, taken aback for a moment, rallied and replied, "I don't rightly know. He's only ten years old. I don't believe he's been fooling with the girls yet."

James Still
MALLIE, KENTUCKY

Stalemate

The school was playing a rival in what appeared to be a hot game, when the English teacher arrived late. She asked a big old boy what the score was. He replied, "Nary one to nary one. Ain't nary one made ary one."

Mary Louise Nadell
NEWPORT, TENNESSEE

Specialization

Student, rushing into the office of his faculty advisor just after mid-terms: "I need help bad."

Professor: "What's your trouble?"

Student: "I just made four Fs and a D."

Professor: "Well, what's your explanation for that?"

Student: "I spent too much time on that one subject."

Dr. Ohmer Milton
ALCOA, TENNESSEE

I Can Handle That

A mountain boy did well in high school and won a scholarship to Harvard. He arrived on campus but had trouble finding his way around. He saw a professor and asked, "Where's the admissions office at?"

Like I said, this was a professor, and he said, "My dear fellow, up here we don't end our sentences with prepositions. Why don't you ask your question again?"

Whereupon the mountaineer said, "Okay. Where's the admissions office at, you jackass?"

Jerry Workman
BEREA, KENTUCKY

A Success

A fellow dropped out of a mountain school and went to Cleveland to get a job. The principal of the school was in Cleveland and found the drop-out owned a whole block. He looked him up, said, "How did you do it?"

"Well," the fellow said, "I started out buying T-shirts for a dollar apiece and selling them for two dollars. You know, if you can keep on making a one percent profit like that, you can get ahead."

Loyal Jones

You Try It

This old boy from back in the country went off to the university, mainly to play basketball. He was good at that but not too good at his studies. After a year, his grades caught up with him, and the dean told him that he'd have to raise his grade average during the next fall semester or he'd be out of school. Hearing of his plight, the coach said, "Why don't you take old Professor Filbert's ornithology course. All you do in there is look at bird films and tramp around in the fields birdwatching. He just gives one exam, and all you have to do is look at slides and identify the birds. You're from the country. You know birds, and you ought to make an A."

So he pre-registered for the course, but during the summer the old professor died, and the university hired a new teacher just out of graduate school. He was ambitious and wanted to establish himself as a hard teacher. He asked his students to read all the books on ornithology in the library, and he assigned a long research paper. For the first exam he strung about thirty pairs of bird legs across the room and asked them to identify the bird from each set of legs and to write about the mating patterns, feeding habits, habitat, and migratory practices of each one. The old boy thought that he recognized the feet of the duck and the hawk, but he wasn't sure about any of the others. He got real upset, jumped up, stomped down to the teacher's desk, threw down his exam and yelled, "This is a terrible test, and you are a terrible teacher! This course is ridiculous!"

This made the young professor mad, and he tried to assert his authority. "What is your name, young man?" he demanded.

The country boy jumped up on the teacher's desk, pulled his pants legs up to his knees, and yelled back, "You tell *me,* doctor!"

Dr. Lee Morris
BEREA, KENTUCKY

Education Is a Good Thing

A one-mule farmer got interested in education and bought himself some vocabulary books. After a few weeks, his neighbors heard him plowing with the following instructions to his mule: "Maude, halt, pivot and proceed."

Becky Nelson
BEREA, KENTUCKY

Lethal Ailment

A chicken farmer noticed that some of his chickens were ailing. He decided to find out what was making them sick. So, he wrung the neck of one of them and mailed it to the agriculture department of the state university. In a week or so, he got a report which read, "Our analysis shows that your chicken died of a broken neck."

Loyal Jones

They Aren't the Same

A young lawyer once asked Dr. Hector Barnett, our veterinarian, how much education he had.

The old man stroked his chin and weighed his answer carefully before he replied. "Well, son, that depends on whether you're talkin' schoolin' or learnin'."

Tom Powell
RICHMOND, KENTUCKY

''Ten Feet Tall and Bullet-Proof'':

MOONSHINE AND OTHER SPIRITS

A Moonshine Game

My Uncle Arlo has a little bottling works up in the hills—makes a drink he calls ''summer vacation.'' Get about two drinks and school is out! It is *strong*. The old boys up home like to play a little game with it. They'll get out about half a pint and sit in a circle out behind the barn, and pass it around to the three of them for about fifteen minutes. Then one will get up and leave. The other two has to try and guess which one it was!

The other day they ran off a new batch and sampled it a lot. You shouldn't do that, because it'll make you feel about ten feet tall and bullet-proof. As soon as he sampled it, Uncle Arlo went straight into town and rented an empty store and started charging people a quarter apiece to come and see the animals and snakes. And he was the only one a-seeing 'em.

People got irritated, said he was taking money under false

pretenses, so they went to get the sheriff to arrest him. When the sheriff got there, Uncle Arlo got to talkin' to him and gave him a couple of drinks, sold him half interest in the store!

Dr. Carl Hurley
LEXINGTON, KENTUCKY

More Than He Could Drink

A man who drank more than was good for him worked on the county road crew. His fellow workers decided to go see the county judge to see if they could get more pay. He said he wasn't interested, but they kept after him until he said he would go with them. When they got there, he stayed in the back and didn't have anything to say. The judge listened to the petition of the road crew and then looked at the reluctant protester and said, ''John, you haven't said anything. Do you think you ought to have a raise?''

''Hell no, Judge,'' he said. ''It's killing me to drink up what I'm making now.''

Mike Mullins
HINDMAN, KENTUCKY

High Achievers

A woman was discussing her two sons, both of whom had stories about them in the weekly newspaper. ''Oh,'' she said, ''I'm so proud of my boys. Johnny was in the paper for making the highest grades in law school and becoming editor of the law review, and Freddy was in there for blowing the highest he ever did on the breathalyzer test.''

Mike Mullins

Strained Whiskey

A golfer went to visit his old friend in the hospital and tried to cheer him up. But the friend, knowing he was close to going on to the great golf course in the sky, restrained him. He preferred to spend their time talking about some memorable rounds and the fun they'd both had at the nineteenth hole, the clubhouse lounge, drinking.

When the golfer was about to leave his sick friend said, "One last request, partner. As soon as I'm buried and they've put the sod in place over me, I want you to come back alone with a fifth of Kentucky's finest and pour it over my grave. Will you do that?"

The golfer, a practical man as well as one of humor, studied a moment, winked at the man, and said, "Sure, I'd be glad to. But if you don't mind, I'll run it through my kidneys first."

Billy Edd Wheeler

Seal of Approval

These two old 'shiners were arguing about who made the best 'shine, so they decided to get scientific about it and send a sample off to the University of Kentucky Extension Service to be tested.

They bottled up the two samples, sent it off, and waited about a week. One of the old-timers got the letter, and he couldn't wait to get down to the other's house. They opened up the letter and read: "Gentlemen: You can work your horses."

John Harrod
OWENTON, KENTUCKY

One-Way Trip

It seems that the cronies of an old man on his deathbed made up enough money to buy themselves a jug of liquor against the day of his burial. They consulted him about whether to open the jug going to the cemetery, or coming back. "Boys," the old man said, "open it goin' out. I won't be with you comin' back."

Allen M. Trout
FRANKFORT, KENTUCKY

Nothing To Look Forward To

I was driving toward Richmond, Kentucky, one day, and I picked up a hitchhiker. We drove along for a while, and I asked him where he was going and why. "Well," he said, "I'm going over to Richmond to get drunk." Then he added, "And I sorta dread it."

Dr. Warren Lambert
BEREA, KENTUCKY

That Clinches It

Counsel to police witness: "But if a man is on his hands and knees in the middle of the road, does that prove he was drunk?"

Policeman: "No, sir, it does not, but this one was trying to roll up the white line."

James Clifford Terry
KNOXVILLE, TENNESSEE

Just Right

A constituent of mine down in North Carolina bought some moonshine liquor during Prohibition days, and he gave it to one of his less affluent friends. Some time thereafter, my constituent asked his friend whether he had drunk the liquor, and his friend said yes, he had. My constituent asked, "Well, what did you think of it?"

He said, "Well, it was just right."

So the donor asked the donee, "What do you mean by the statement that the liquor was just right?"

He said, "I mean that if it had been any better, you

wouldn't have given it to me, and if it had been any worse, I couldn't have drunk it."

Sen. Sam J. Ervin, Jr.
MORGANTON, NORTH CAROLINA

Honest Mistake

A drunk, already wobbly, went into a tavern and asked for a drink, which the bartender provided. Directly he called out, "Hey, bartender, do your lemons have legs?"

"Of course not," the bartender answered.

"Well, in that case," the man said, "I have just squeezed your canary into my drink."

Glenn Baker
FAIRMONT, WEST VIRGINIA

Sterling Performance

A little boy told his neighbor, "My daddy got arrested for drunken driving!"

The neighbor said, "Well, John, where were you?"

"Well," said the boy, "we was over in Judyville. Cartwright pulled him over and made him get out, pick up a dime, walk the white line, touch his toe to the bumper, and all."

The neighbor said, "That's hard to do—how'd he do?"

John said, "He done pretty good to be as drunk as he was."

Charles Tribble
CYNTHIANA, KENTUCKY

Being Practical

The revenue officers came by this house in the mountains and asked a small boy where his daddy was. "Making whiskey," the boy said.

"Where?"

"I'll show you for ten dollars," the boy said.

"Okay, let's go."

"Pay me first."

"No, we'll pay you when we get back," the revenuer said.

"You ain't coming back," the boy retorted.

Jim Ralston
PAINT LICK, KENTUCKY, and PARADISE VALLEY, ARIZONA

The Wages of Sin

This man got bad to drink, and when he got drunk, he got sick and it took him a few days to get over it. His wife was worried about him and nagged him a lot. One day she said that if he didn't quit drinking that he was going to puke his guts up and that would be the end of him. A few days later she killed a chicken, picked it outside, and brought it to the kitchen sink to clean it. She left its entrails in the sink while she prepared the chicken for the frying pan, got it on, and went outside to do something or other. Her husband had been drinking, lying on the couch, and he got real sick. He rushed to the sink and threw up. In a few minutes his wife came in and found him in deep distress, weeping and wailing. He threw his arms around her neck and said, "You were right, honey. I threw up my guts, but with the grace of God and a long-handled spoon, I got them back down again!"

Bob Sears
SOMERSET, KENTUCKY

The Drunk and the One-Eyed Cat

A hillbilly in the advanced stages of inebriation entered the East Tennessee Bar and ordered a drink. The bartender saw the glaze in his eyes and told him he'd had enough,

but the drunk insisted he was not drunk and demanded a drink. "All right," the bartender said, "if you're not drunk, tell me what that is in the doorway over yonder."

The drunk looked, said, "It's a one-eyed cat coming in."

"Nope, I told you you were drunk. That cat is going out!"

Billy Edd Wheeler

Christmas Spirits

The man had spent some time at the spiked wassail bowl before his church group went out caroling.

"Leon, Leon," he sang blithely, his red nose glowing.

His wife nudged him and whispered in his ear, "Honey, you're holding your book upside-down. It's 'Noel, Noel'!"

Billy Edd Wheeler

Whatever It Was, He Liked It

A drunk wandered into a bar to have one last drink before going home and noticed a lot of people gathered around a dart board. "Whassh goin' on?" he asked the bartender.

"We've got a contest going," said the bartender. "If you hit the bull's-eye you get a prize. Wanna try?"

"Sure," said the drunk, whereupon he tossed the dart and, lo and behold, hit the bull's-eye. So he was awarded the prize, which was a live turtle about the size of a large biscuit.

Several weeks later the drunk happened into the same bar where another contest was underway, so he tossed the dart and miraculously hit the bull's-eye again. The bartender looked him over, said, "Weren't you in here a while back, and didn't you win a prize then?"

"Sh-sh-shure did."

"Well, we have different prizes and I don't want to give you the same one you won last time. So tell me, what *did* you win the last time?"

The drunk thought a minute, scratched his head, said, "I think it was a roast beef sandwich on a r-r-real hard bun."

Billy Edd Wheeler

Drinking for his Buddy

A well-dressed man started coming into the lounge at the Great Smokies Hilton, where he would always order two drinks at a time. Two scotches and water.

After a few weeks of this the bartender's curiosity got the best of him, so he asked the man about it, said, "Why don't you just order doubles?"

"Tell you the truth, it's a sentimental thing," the man told him. "A while back my best buddy died in the hospital. Before he died we spent a lot of time talking about the good times we'd had, the fishing trips we'd taken, the golf we'd played, and how much fun we'd had drinking together. He made me promise that every now and then I'd drink a drink for him, just for old times' sake."

The bartender thought that was nice, but for a few weeks he didn't see the man. Then one night he came in and ordered one scotch and water.

"But what about your dead buddy?" the bartender asked. "Aren't you going to have one for him?"

"This is his drink right here," the man said, "I'm on the wagon."

He drank the drink and said, "Let me have one more for him. A promise is a promise, you know, and, shucks, I know he'd do it for me. Yep, just one more, and then I've got to get on home.''

Billy Edd Wheeler

"More Particular, Less Desirable":

OLD AGE

Diminishing Prospects

One old bachelor to another: "How's it going, Fred?"

"Not too good. As I get older I get more particular and less desirable."

Dr. John Ramsay
BEREA, KENTUCKY

Matter of Economics

An elderly couple came to see a small-town doctor and said that they would like to use one of his examining rooms, would be glad to pay the twenty-five-dollar fee. The doctor didn't have all that many patients, so he said all right. But they came back the next week, asked the same thing, and the next week also. Well, the doctor got to worrying about this thing, medical ethics and all, so he asked them why they were coming to the clinic. The old man explained, "Well, Doc, we're married, but not to each other. If we go to a motel, we have to pay thirty dollars. If we come here, we get eighteen dollars back from Medicare."

Harry M. Caudill
WHITESBURG, KENTUCKY

Don't Rush Me

Two elderly gentlemen were sitting on a bench in front of the feed store. "I think I know you," one said to the other. "What's your name?"

"Do you have to know right now?" the other replied.

Carol Elizabeth Reynolds
RABUN GAP, GEORGIA

Wrinkled

An elderly woman moved into a small town, and she got a crush on the druggist. He and the grocer, shoe repairman, insurance man, and others would spend a great part of each working day sitting on benches in front of their establishments. This woman would go by and try to engage the druggist in conversation, but he paid little attention to her. One day she thought to herself, "I'll make him notice me." So she took off all of her clothes and streaked past the loafers on their bench.

They stared at her and were quiet for a while. Then one said, "What was that?"

"I don't know," said the druggist, "but whatever it was needs pressing."

Lily Bennett McGinty
PROSPECT, KENTUCKY

Faulty Memory

A fellow was walking down the street when he saw an old man sitting on a park bench just crying his eyes out. "What's the matter, old fellow?" he asked.

"I just got married to this beautiful young woman," he said. "She loves me, and I love her, and we have a wonderful time. I have this beautiful house and a yard with flowers and anything I want."

"Well, then why are you crying like that?"

"I can't remember where I live."

Betty Jane Isaac Smith
FRANKFORT, KENTUCKY

Connected

Roy Acuff to Grandpa Jones on Ralph Emory's "Nashville Now" (both with clip-on microphones and Grandpa with a hearing aid): "Are you ready, Grandpa?"

"Yeah, I'm hooked up like the TVA."

Louis Marshall "Grandpa" Jones
MOUNTAIN VIEW, ARKANSAS

Cautious

When someone asked me whether or not I was investing in the stock market, I told him, "No, at my age, I don't even buy green bananas."

Dr. Thomas D. Clark
LEXINGTON, KENTUCKY

He Almost Shot His Age

Elwood Honnicker was a hard-luck kind of guy, but today he was high as a kite. He was having the best round of golf of his life. He had always dreamed of shooting his age and today he would do it, if he only sank a two-foot putt. He was seventy-five years old and he was lying seventy-four.

The putt was not that hard. It was dead level. But Elwood surveyed it from every angle, plummed it with his putter, studied the grain between the ball and the hole. Twice he stood over the ball and almost putted, then backed away to collect himself. The longer he waited the more nervous he became. His heart was pounding in his chest. Finally he stood over the ball, slowly started back with his putter—and fell over dead. Heart attack.

He was cremated. After the church service his ashes were taken to the eighteenth green where, according to his wishes, they were to be scattered. Just as the urn was tilted and the ashes started to pour forth, a wind came up and blew him out of bounds!

Billy Edd Wheeler

Get Serious

At a teachers' meeting to which the county retired teachers were invited to learn about their benefits programs, a man from the retirement system was explaining why they ought to require the women to pay more than the men. "For example," he said, "for every man of eighty, there are two women of that age or older."

"Sir," said an old man who hadn't been listening too carefully, "I'm eighty-nine years old, and that's about the most useless information you could have given me."

Loyal Jones

Guessing His Age

There were two folks in the nursing home, a man and a woman. He said, "Betcha can't guess how old I am."

She said, "Take your clothes off and I'll tell you."

So he undressed.

She said, "You're seventy-six years old."

He marveled, "How'd you know that?"

"You told me about two hours ago!"

Glenn Baker
FAIRMONT, WEST VIRGINIA

A Bad Memory

Aunt Mavis and Uncle Arlo, they're getting up in years now, but they was sitting out on the porch the other evening just rocking. She said, "You know what I'd like to have?"

He said, "What?"

She said, "A big bowl of vanilla ice cream."

He said, "Boy, that *would* be good."

She said, "A big bowl of vanilla ice cream with chocolate syrup on it!"

He got up and started off. "I'll go down to the drugstore and get us some."

She said, "Now, that's vanilla ice cream with syrup on it—write it down."

He said, "I don't need to write it down. I can remember that."

About forty-five minutes later he was back with two ham sandwiches. She said, as he handed her one of them and she looked into it, "You dummy, I told you to write it down. I wanted mustard on mine!"

Dr. Carl Hurley
LEXINGTON, KENTUCKY

It Gets Away from You

An oral historian was talking with an old man and asked him if he remembered events from a bygone era in which he was interested. The old man said, "Why, I remember those days as if they were yesterday."

A little way into the interview, the historian discovered that he didn't remember much of anything. Exasperated, he exclaimed, "I thought you told me that you remember these things as if they were yesterday."

"Well, I do," the man said. "But I don't remember much of what happened yesterday either."

Dr. Thomas R. Ford
LEXINGTON, KENTUCKY

The Drawbacks of Ageing

This old man was walking along the golf course, and there were three guys standing there ready to tee off, but the fourth had not shown up. So they asked the old man if he'd like to play a little golf with them. He said, "Well, sure, I've played a little golf." They said that they played a fast game, but he said he'd give it a try. They also said that they played for money, but he said that was all right.

So they played nine holes and he beat them like a drum, won a lot of money. They played a second nine holes and he beat them again. Wanted to play a third round, but they said they wanted to go to the clubhouse and do some drinking. He said, "Okay," and proceeded to drink them under the table!

One of them asked, "Look, old fellow, you beat us at golf, you took all our money, and you drank us under the table. Doesn't old age have any disadvantages at all?"

The old man thought for a minute and said, "Yeah, I can think of one. This morning when I woke up I asked my wife to make love, and she said, 'What, after seven times last night?' You see, when you get old, your *memory* starts to slip a little!"

John Vickery
and William Lightfoot
BOONE, NORTH CAROLINA

Let There Be Light

The old man was finishing up with his physical and, except for bad eyesight, the doctor pronounced him fit. All during the physical the old man was carrying on about how his life had changed since he had been born again.

"Why, it's got so that when I get up in the night to go to the bathroom, sometimes the Lord turns on the light for me. It's a miracle."

As the old man was getting dressed the doctor chatted with his wife, said, "What's this he tells me about the Lord turning on the lights for him?"

"Oh, goodness," she said, concerned. "Has he been going potty in the refrigerator again!"

Billy Edd Wheeler

The Best Way to Die

Three senior gentlemen of Appalachia were wisecracking one day, covering a host of subjects, when the talk turned to the most desirable way of dying. The first man, a racing fan, age seventy-five, thought the ideal way to go would be to crash in a car going a hundred miles per hour. The second man, an aviation nut, age eighty-seven, said he would like to crash in a jet plane going nine hundred miles an hour. The third man, age ninety-five, said, "I'd like to die in the arms of a beautiful blonde—shot by her jealous husband."

Billy Edd Wheeler

Dressed for Heaven

A stingy old woman told her neighbor, "Now when I die, cut the back out of my dress—don't waste all that material. My husband is already dead."

Her neighbor said, "You don't want to cut the back out of your dress, because when you walk up to the Golden Gate with your husband, why, that just wouldn't look right."

She said, "Aw, don't worry about it—I buried my husband without his pants!"

Glenn Baker
FAIRMONT, WEST VIRGINIA

Senior Exercise

The local newspaper sent a reporter around to interview the old man who had an important birthday coming up. "Tell me, sir," the reporter began, "what exercise do you do to keep fit at your age? I hear you're pushing ninety."

"Son," the old man said, "when you're pushing ninety that's all the exercise you need."

Billy Edd Wheeler

The following anonymous collection has been printed, reprinted, added to, and shared widely.

You Know You're Getting Old When

Everything hurts, and what doesn't hurt doesn't work

The gleam in your eye is the sun hitting your bifocals

Your knees buckle, but your belt won't

You feel like the night before, and you haven't been anywhere

You sit down in a rocking chair, and you can't get it started

Your little black book contains only names ending in M.D.

Your back goes out more than you do

You know all the answers, but nobody asks you the questions

Your children begin to look middle-aged

Your mind makes contracts your body can't keep

You finally get it all together but can't remember where you put it

You have more hair on your chest than on your head

You turn out the lights for economic rather than romantic reasons

The best part of your day is over when the alarm clock goes off

It takes you an hour to undress and another to remember why

Your midnight oil is all used up by nine o'clock

You get your exercise from being pallbearer to friends who exercised

Any change you drop less than a quarter isn't worth bending over for

The little old lady you help across the street is your wife

Dialing long distance wears you out

You just can't stand people who are intolerant

You sink your teeth into a steak and they stay there

You finally get to the top of the ladder but it's leaning against the wrong wall.

HYMN
Today's Sermon
The Devil in our Community

''Love in My Heart, But Hell in My Britches'':

RELIGION

Hot Pants

My mother used to tell this one about a circuit-rider, and I relate to it because my grandfather was a circuit-rider. They'd go around and preach at different churches, and they'd usually stay at a house next to the church. Sometimes they would leave an extra suit in the house. This circuit-rider had left a suit in the smokehouse. They were having a late fall revival, and he went into the smokehouse to change and then went directly into the church where they had built up a big fire—had the church good and hot. Now, what he didn't know was that there was a wasp's nest in his pants. He started his sermon, began sweating and then squirming. All of a sudden he ran down the isle and screamed, ''I've got love in my heart but hell in my britches!''

Billy Wilson
BEREA, KENTUCKY

A Special Passenger

Don Jennings was listening to his friend tell him about a terrible accident he'd just had. Don couldn't believe it. He said, "Now, let me get this straight, Lonzo. You say you flipped your car over at Buzzard's Bend, rolled down the hill, over the cliff, crashed onto the rocks a hundred and fifty feet below where the car burst into flames—and you walked away from the crash without a scratch?"

"Yup," Lonzo said, a sort of dense grin on his face, like it was something that happened to him every day. No big deal.

Don shook his head and whistled in disbelief, said, "All I can say is the Lord must've been with you."

"No," Lonzo replied, seriously, "it was Fuzzy Price."

Billy Edd Wheeler

Hard Work in Heaven

Charlie Stafford, my fix-it man friend who lives over there in Black Mountain, North Carolina, took me fishing down at Lake James the other day and all he could talk about was the dream he'd had. Said it worried him. He talks real country, Charlie does, can make Gomer and Barney and Festus sound like urbanites.

"Billy Bob," he said, "las' night I dreamed I died. 'Stead o' goin' up yander I went down thar. I ain't been thar but a few days when the telemaphone rings, and I answers, and I says, who's this-hyar a-talkin'? And he says, 'This-hyar's Ronnie, Ronnie Solesby.' And I says, 'Ronnie, where you at?' And he says back at me, 'I's up-hyar in heaven.' Then he wants to know how it is down thar where I'm at?

"'Ain't too bad,' says I, 'ain't too bad a-tall. All I gotta do is shovel a leetle coal now and again. Then I toast my feets while I's restin' my bones and mostly takes the rest o' the day off. You see, ain't enough work to go around down here, so we kinda spread it around. I only work a couple o' hours a day. By the by, Ronnie, says I, how's the work up-thar in heaven?'

"'Charlie,' he says, 'hit's work, work, work, all the time

up here. Don't never git no rest. I git up every mornin' at three-thirty and we take in the stars and the moon. Then we hang out the sun and push clouds 'round all day. I'm tellin' you, Charlie, hit's a workshop, and it ain't union neither. Ain't no nine-to-five stuff.'

"I says, 'Ronnie, what in the world's a-matter? How come you got to work so hard up-thar in heaven?'

"He says, 'Well, we're short o' help.'"

Billy Edd Wheeler
(from Riley Wilson)

The Devil Goes to Church

We got to wanting to have a masquerade party. We'd heard about them and they sounded like fun. So we decided to have one and we picked out a fellow's house and we were going to meet at his house on Halloween and have that party.

He lived way out in the country and I had to walk a long ways. I dressed up like the Devil and started down the road, but a rainstorm came up and I needed a place to get in out of the weather. So I darted into a little building by the side of the road.

It just so happened it was a little country church, and they were right in the midst of a big revival meeting! Law, you can imagine what a commotion it caused when I jumped up in the door, with my red Devil outfit on, my horns on the top of my head and my pitchfork in my hand!

They went out of doors and windows—any way to get out. One old boy up toward the front jumped up to run, but got his coattail caught in the seat and couldn't get away. He wheeled around and throwed up both arms and said, "I've been a member of this church for going on twenty-five years, but I've been on *your* side all along!"

Dr. Carl Hurley
LEXINGTON, KENTUCKY

Jesus and the College President

There was a man walking down the road, limping, and he met the Master. Jesus asked, "Brother, what's your problem?'' The man said, ''Well, I'm lame.'' Jesus reached out and touched him and made him whole and he went away happy.

The second man came down this road, stumbling and falling, and met Jesus, who again asked, ''Brother what is your problem?'' He said, ''I'm blind.'' Jesus reached out and touched him and he became whole again; he could see and he went down the road, happy.

A third man came down the road weeping uncontrollably, and met the Master. Jesus asked, ''Brother, what is *your* problem?'' The man said, ''I'm a new college president.'' And Jesus sat down and wept with him!

Dr. John Stephenson,
President of Berea College
BEREA, KENTUCKY

Easy to Recognize

A guy died and went to heaven. St. Peter was showing him around, and the guy thought it was wonderful. It was great—a beautiful place, just paradise. They went around the corner, and there was a bunch of people in chains, and the guy asked St. Peter why in the world these people were chained. St. Peter replied, ''That's a bunch of hillbillies, and every Friday at 5:00 p.m., they want to head home for the weekend!''

William E. Lightfoot
BOONE, NORTH CAROLINA

Miraculous Golf

Moses and Jesus were playing a round of golf on one of the harder heavenly links and were trying to one-up each other performing miracles as they played. Moses got thirsty and since there were no water fountains around, he struck a rock and water poured forth. Jesus got hungry, found a morsel of bread in his golf bag, made it multiply into enough for a snack for him and Moses.

Once Moses hit into a big lake. Instead of taking a penalty and teeing up another ball, he told Jesus, ''Watch this.'' He waved his arms, the water parted, he walked to his ball and hit it out of the dry lake bed.

Soon after that Jesus hit his ball into the lake, said, "Watch this," and started to walk on top of the water out to his ball. But he sank. He walked out all wet and shaking his head, said, "I don't understand it. I used to be able to do that."

"Yeah, but remember," Moses said, "that was before you had holes in your feet."

Billy Edd Wheeler

There's One in Every Crowd

The Sunday School teacher told her little ones the story of the Prodigal Son who came home, whose father was so glad to see him he killed the fatted calf and threw a real party, and how everyone was full of joy, except for the older brother who was jealous of the attention being given his brother.

Later the teacher was quizzing them about the story, and she asked, "Who was not happy about all this?"

A little boy spoke up. "The really unhappy one was the fatted calf!"

Howard E. Stanton
SWANNANOA, NORTH CAROLINA

The Lord Can Only Do So Much

This old fellow way down in the mountains, poor ole Uncle Bill, was sitting there on the porch a-whittling during one of the awfulest floods you ever heard of. That river was just a-rolling, and the rains were coming down terribly. A boat came by and a man hollered, "Come on, brother Bill, get in the boat! The floods are a-coming and you're going to drown!"

Bill said, "The good Lord will take care of me." And he just went on whittling.

Another boat came by and a man spied Uncle Bill on top of his house, sitting there a-whittling. He hollered, "Get in here, Bill, and go with us!"

"No, sir," replied Uncle Bill, "the good Lord will take care of me."

In a few minutes they came by in a helicopter and there was poor ole Uncle Bill hugging the chimney, and they said, "Get in here quick, so we can save you!"

He said, "No sir, the Lord's taking care of me." About that time the house washed down the river.

Uncle Bill landed in heaven. He looked at St. Peter and he asked, "What'd you let me down for?"

St. Peter replied, "Don't you come up here and cause no trouble. We sent two boats and a helicopter after you!"

"Old Joe" Clark
BEREA, KENTUCKY

Why Me, Lord?

A bearded long-haired guy, not too familiar with baths, saw this gorgeous girl and immediately fell in love with her. He asked her to go out with him, and she refused, with some disdain. He rushed to a barber shop, got a haircut and a shave, went out and bought a new suit, shirt, tie, shoes and everything. He got all dressed up, sought out the girl again, asked for a date, and she agreed. He drove to her house, went to her front door, ushered her out to the car, opened the door for her, and as he was walking around the car to get in, lightning struck him. As he lay in the street, dazed, unable to move, he weakly asked, "Why me, Lord, and why now?"

A voice came down from the sky: "Is that you, Sam? Sorry, I didn't recognize you."

James "Pop" Hollandsworth
ASHEVILLE, NORTH CAROLINA

Wet Cheese

The little boy was on his way home with some groceries from the company store when he slipped in a mud puddle and yelled, "Jesus Christ, God almighty!"

The Baptist preacher heard him, ran over and grabbed him by the arm, said, "What did you say, young man?"

Thinking fast, the boy said, "Cheese and crackers got all muddy!"

Billy Edd Wheeler

A Sin a Second

When his day came old Joe found himself at the gates of heaven, where St. Peter greeted him and allowed him to enter. As they were walking along they came upon this huge hallway that seemed miles long. It was full of shelves, which held boxes that resembled clocks with hands. Each one had a name and there were millions of them.

Old Joe asked St. Peter, "What are all these boxes with names on them?"

"Each one of these boxes tells us when a person sins," St. Peter said. "Every time those hands move, well, it means that that person has committed a sin."

Old Joe started looking around and, sure enough, he found his friend Henry's name. Henry's clock was ticking and ticking away. Over there was Jim's clock. Jim's wasn't moving too fast. Then he thought about a friend called Dirty Sam. Dirty Sam was known in their small town by nearly everyone, for he was always drinking and cussing and telling dirty jokes to anyone that would listen.

But he looked and looked and couldn't find Dirty Sam's clock. So he asked St. Peter, "Where is Dirty Sam's clock? Surely he's around here somewhere."

St Peter said, "Well, it's been a little warm up here lately, so we moved his clock into the main office and we're using it for a fan."

Michael E. Hogan
HOMOSASSA SPRINGS, FLORIDA

Unimpressed

The deacon was proud of the new minister, and he could hardly wait to tell his neighbor, a skeptical farmer, about him. "He's got a B.S., an M.S., and a Ph.D."

"Well, I'm not much on these educated preachers," the farmer said. "We all know what B.S. stands for. M.S. means 'more of the same' and Ph.D. means 'piled higher and deeper.'"

Buddy Westbrook
LONDON, KENTUCKY

If You Don't Mind

A preacher was visiting a critically ill member of his congregation who was in the hospital. He crept dolefully up to his bedside and asked, "Is there anything I can do for you, Brother Johnson?"

"Yes," wheezed Mr. Johnson, "you can get your foot off my oxygen tube."

Loyal Jones

Seeds Worth Saving

The hotel was catering two dinners at once, one to a group of clergymen from all over Appalachia, the other to a group of liquor distributors and wholesale dealers. The liquor people ordered a special dessert: watermelon soaked with brandy, rum, and Benedictine.

The catering manager discovered to his chagrin that there had been a mixup. The spiked melon had been served by mistake to the ministers. He reported this to the general manager, who asked him, "Were there any complaints? What did the ministers say?"

"They didn't say a word," he said. "They were too busy putting the seeds from the melon into their pockets."

Billy Edd Wheeler

Worse Than He Thought

The little boy noticed a plaque in the back of the church and asked the preacher what it was. "Oh, those are the church members who died in service," he explained.

"Which," the boy asked, "the ten o'clock or the eleven o'clock one?"

Dr. Michael Nichols
LEXINGTON, KENTUCKY

The Preacher Ran Away

An old fellow died and he was stooped over pretty bad, so he had to be strapped down in his casket. It was placed in the small country church during the funeral services. Well, it got so hot, the elastic strap broke and the corpse sat up. The church cleared out—everybody.

About two or three days later a couple of old men said, ''Well, I don't know about our preacher. He may not be quite what he oughta be.''

The other one said, ''Yeah, the other day when he passed me, a-running for all he was worth, I heard him say, 'Damn a church with only one door in it!'''

Billy Edd Wheeler

Honest Mistake

The preacher had been invited to dinner at the home of parishioners, and he was seated by the hostess. He had a glass of wine, to which he was unaccustomed. Halfway through the meal he turned to his hostess and said, ''I don't want to alarm you, but I think I'm paralyzed. I've been squeezing my leg for about five minutes, and I can't feel a thing.''

''Oh, don't worry,'' she said, ''that's *my* leg you've been squeezing.''

Loyal Jones

Not Enough To Go Around

The Sunday School teacher was showing her class a picture of Daniel in the lions' den, when a little boy began to cry. She hastened to reassure him by saying that God would save Daniel. ''But that little one in the corner's not going to get any,'' the little boy sobbed.

Loyal Jones

Coming Attractions

Radio preacher: Do you want to learn what hell is? Tune in next week. We'll be featuring our organist.

Dr. Michael Nichols
LEXINGTON, KENTUCKY

Bluegrass Heaven

A bluegrass music fan died and went to heaven. He was met at the gate by St. Peter, who asked what part of heaven he would like to see first. So he asked if there was a bluegrass section. St. Peter said there was and that he would be glad to show it to him. They walked over a hill to a beautiful pastoral place. It had a few campers up on the hills and three buses that wouldn't start, looked just like what the fan was used to. He looked around and then noticed a man sitting on the hood of a car with a Martin D-45 guitar, playing and singing "White Dove."

"Why, that's Carter Stanley," he said, overjoyed.

"Yes," said St. Peter, "that's Carter."

He walked a little farther and saw two fellows playing "Salty Dog."

"Isn't that Lester Flatt and Paul Warren?" he asked, really excited.

"That's right," said St. Peter. "They're here."

Then he saw a man in a big white hat with gray hair all around his ears, sitting on a stump playing "Rawhide" on a mandolin. That made him sad. "Don't tell me that Bill Monroe is dead," he said.

"Oh, no," said St. Peter, "that's God. He just thinks he's Bill Monroe."

Susan Jones
BLACK MOUNTAIN, NORTH CAROLINA

Wrong Time

Years ago when the northern lights were especially bright in Kentucky, a young man went out late one night, saw them and thought it was the end of time. He rushed down through the community, trying to wake people up. He came to the house of an old man, started pounding on his door, yelling, "Get up! The Day of Judgment has come!"

The old man yelled back, "Go back to bed. Who ever heard of the Day of Judgment coming in the middle of the night?"

Hilde Capps
BEREA, KENTUCKY

Not a Smidgen of That Here

A devout woman saved up for a trip to London so she could see St. Paul's Cathedral, which she had heard about. She arrived in London and went to church at St. Paul's on Sunday. She had never seen or heard anything so beautiful. The organ pealed, the choirs sang, and the whole thing was wonderful to her. She got so excited she jumped up and shouted, "Glory hallelujah!"

An usher in a cutaway coat came quickly down the isle and said, "Madam, we don't allow outbursts here!"

"I can't help it," she said. "I've got religion."

The usher drew himself up and said stiffly, "Well, you didn't get it here!"

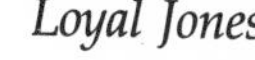

Loyal Jones

Biblical Inerrancy

A visitor to east Tennessee, noting that the three wise men in a church nativity play scene were dressed in firemen's coats and hats, asked why. In his clear east Tennessee dialect, a church member responded, "Don't you know what the Bible says? It says they came from a-far."

Dr. Estill P. Muncy
JEFFERSON CITY, TENNESSEE

No Reflection on You

A man got up in the middle of the pastor's sermon and walked out. After church, his embarrassed wife sought to explain to the preacher. "I hope you don't think he disagreed with what you said. He just has a tendency to walk in his sleep."

Dr. Charles S. Webster
NAPLES, FLORIDA

Watch That Grammar

St. Peter was standing at the Pearly Gates watching an assistant check in new arrivals. The assistant had a roster and was calling out names as the spirits lined up. "James Robertson," he read off, and a fellow said, "I'm him." Then he read "William Bumgarner," and another fellow said, "That's me." Then he read, "Gladys Humphreys," and a woman answered, "I am she." St. Peter leaned over and whispered to his assistant, "Another damn schoolteacher."

Loyal Jones

Uncertain Pedigree

This unmarried woman had three sets of twins, two, four, and six years old. She got in desperate shape and went to the welfare office to get some help. She filled out the forms and sat down with a social worker for an interview. "Do you have a husband?" the social worker asked.

"No, ain't never had one."

"Well, who is the father of your children?"

"It depends on which ones you're talking about."

"All right, let's start with the two-year-old twins. Who's their father?"

"Well, I hate to tell you, but it was the preacher down at the valley church."

"What about the four-year-olds?"

"Now, that was the former preacher."

"All right, who is the father of the six-year-olds?"

"Oh my, them two. Ain't they handsome fellows? I just don't know who they belong to. They 'as born before I got religion."

Mabel Martin Wyrick
CORBIN, KENTUCKY

Stretching Your Money

Question: "How do you make copper wire?"
Answer: "Give two Methodists a penny."

Frank Vermillion
WINCHESTER, KENTUCKY

Watch the Metaphor

The preacher was waxing eloquent at the funeral of a departed church member. He concluded by saying, "What we have here is just the shell. The nut has gone on."

Rev. Herbert Banks
UZ, KENTUCKY

Prayer Answered

An old couple had a little dog that disappeared one day, and they looked and looked for it but couldn't find it. In a few days the woman went to the sorghum crock to get a pitcher full and found the little dog in there, drowned. Now they were very poor, had little to eat, so they fished the dog out and buried it, then knelt down and prayed that the sorghum wouldn't be ruined. As the woman later reported, "We et that sorghum all winter and there was nary a hair."

Ann Stephenson
BEREA, KENTUCKY

A Bargain

A man and his son went to church, and they came out and the man was complaining that the service was too long, the preacher no good, and the singing off-key. Finally the little boy said, "Daddy, I thought it was pretty good for a dime."

Billy Wilson
BEREA, KENTUCKY

A Believer

This fellow said that his grandmother was so hooked on the TV soap operas that when one of the characters got sick, she'd stand up in church and ask for prayers for them.

Dr. Charles L. Cox
OAK RIDGE, TENNESSEE

The Bible Says . . .

A boy went to his father and asked him to buy him a car. His father said that he would have to earn it. If he went to church every Sunday, read his Bible every day, had perfect attendance in school and kept a 3.0 average, and if he kept his hair cut, he'd buy him a car. In six months the boy said, "I've gone to church every Sunday, read my Bible every day, haven't missed a day of school, and I have better than a 3.0 average." His father said, "Yes, but you haven't kept your hair cut."

The boy replied, "In reading the Bible every day, I found out that Jesus never cut his hair."

"Yeah," his father said, "and if you read your Bible, you know that Jesus had to walk everywhere he went."

Bill Robinson
RICHMOND, KENTUCKY

A Mystery

A man stayed home while his wife went to church. When she returned, he inquired about the sermon. She said it was okay. "Well, what did the preacher preach about?" he persisted.

"I don't know," she said, "he never did say."

Loyal Jones

Abstinence

Three couples, one elderly, one middle-aged, and one young, went to a Catholic church and asked the priest if they could join. "We're under new rules now," he said. "This may seem harsh, but you will have to abstain from sex for a month, and then come back and see me."

So all three couples came back in a month, and the priest asked them how they had done. The elderly couple spoke up first. "It wasn't too bad. We played shuffleboard, took long walks in populated areas, gardened a lot, and slept in twin beds."

"It was harder for us," said the middle-aged couple, "but we kept busy, did some hiking, and when we gardened, one of us worked in the front of the yard and the other in the back, and we also slept in twin beds."

The young man reported, "We did all right the first three weeks by sleeping in separate rooms, just keeping out of each other's way, working hard, and that sort of thing, but one day we were reaching for some vegetables, and I grabbed a cabbage and she picked up a carrot. Our hands touched, and we just couldn't control ourselves."

The priest shook his head and said, "Well, I'm sorry that you young folks won't be able to join the church, but we have to stick to our rules."

"I was afraid of that," the young woman said, "and they won't let us back into Kroger's either."

Rodger Mason
BEREA, KENTUCKY

Commandments

The preacher was teaching the men's Sunday school class on the subject of the Ten Commandments. When he discussed the Eighth Commandment, a man on the front row became distracted and agitated, but when he backed up to the Seventh, the man relaxed and started paying attention again. The preacher saw the man after class and asked if anything was wrong. "Oh, no, preacher, it's all right. When you mentioned the one about stealing, I got upset because I've been thinking that somebody had taken my umbrella, but when you got to the other one about adultery, I remembered where I left it.''

Loyal Jones

Cooks

A famous professor of homiletics from a leading seminary had been invited to a small college to deliver the baccalaureate address. The college president was a trifle nervous in his presence, and when he went to introduce him, he announced that he was professor of home economics, rather than homiletics. After the august person's sermon, the president profusely apologized. ''Oh, that's all right. The jobs are about the same. I have to cook up something every Sunday.''

Martin Ambrose
SAN MORENO, CALIFORNIA

The Farmer and the Lord

A farmer bought a farm at auction, got a good deal, but it was the most run-down, depressing sight he'd ever seen. Grown up with weeds and underbrush, scarred by years of erosion, it was in sad shape. But the farmer was determined to make something of it. He pitched in, cut the weeds, bush-hogged the bushes and shintangle, filled in the gullies, made irrigation dams, fertilized and cultivated the fields until, after two years, he had it looking very respectable.

The local preacher decided to come out for a visit, in connection with the church's fund drive to build a new wing for the Sunday School. He surveyed the apple orchard, the lush green pastures, corn fields, and newly painted barns with a look of wonder. He smiled a smile as wide as the gates of heaven, said, ''Brother, it sure is wonderful to see what you and the Lord have done with this place!''

''Yeah,'' replied the farmer, ''and you should have seen it when the Lord had it by Hisself!''

Billy Edd Wheeler

Step Back, Gabriel

A rural preacher, whose regular job was butchering, had quite a Sunday morning following. His oratorical gifts were known and appreciated all over the county, especially his vivid and poetic portrayal of Gabriel blowing his horn on Judgment Day, waking the faithful from their sleep and calling them home to heaven.

Two bold teenage boys, after hearing the preacher end his sermon week after week talking about Gabriel, decided to play a joke on him. They got a bugle and hid in the church attic just above the pulpit one Sunday.

When the preacher got to the end of his sermon, he said, "And someday, brothers and sisters, Gabriel will blow his mighty trumpet, calling his sheep to the fold. And what a sound it will be, sweeter than the sweetest dulcimer sounds imaginable, yet mighty and triumphal, cutting through the clear air of heaven with majestic, victorious tones. I can hear it now. Listen—can you hear it? Blow, Gabriel, blow!"

At that moment one boy in the attic raised the bugle and blew. The preacher froze. The congregation was startled, looked up. The other boy grabbed for the bugle, wanting to get in on the fun, but the first boy wouldn't let go. He wanted to blow it again. As he pulled back from the grabbing hands of his buddy, pressing his lips to the mouthpiece, blowing another blast, he fell between the ceiling joists and crashed down through drywall and plaster, landing on his feet right in front of the petrified preacher. He had a chalky, ghostly look about him from the dusting of plaster, and his bugle gleamed like bright gold as it caught the morning sun through the window behind the pulpit.

The preacher came to his senses in a split second, reached

into his pocket and pulled out a long switchblade knife, a real hog-sticker, flashed it menacingly at the boy, and yelled, "Step back, Gabriel, or I'll *cut* you!"

Billy Edd Wheeler

It Happened in Heaven

One day in heaven Jesus' secretary walked into his office and said, "Sir, now look, I think you've been working too hard. I don't mean to be bossy but I think you ought to slow down, do a little PR, get out and press the flesh among your people—let them see you and get to know you. I think it would do you a world of good."

Jesus agreed, saved everything he'd worked out on his huge state-of-the-art Super Univac computer, closed his file drawers, and started walking down the streets of gold. He was having a great time, shaking hands, swapping stories, signing autographs. Then from a side street he heard a steady rip-saw, rip-saw noise and upon closer examination saw sawdust floating out of a window. He walked to the window. Inside he saw a bearded carpenter working at his carpenter's bench in a fever, his face dripping perspiration, his hands and arms covered with sawdust.

Jesus walked inside. "Sir," he said in that calm, resonant voice, "why do you labor so? This is heaven—your reward. You can rest here and take it easy. Your days of hard labor and toil are behind you."

"If you don't mind I'll keep on sawing," the man said, "and I'll tell you why. You see, I had a son on earth whose birth was a miracle. I haven't seen him since he died. Now, he knew I was a carpenter, and, my eyesight not being what it used to be, and heaven being such a large place, I figured it might take me an eternity to find him. But I thought if I made enough noise doing my carpentry work, he might hear it and find *me*."

A look of recognition came upon Jesus' face, and the carpenter saw it and stopped sawing. He stared at Jesus quizzically, his eyes beginning to mist with wonder and awe. Their eyes locked.

Jesus said, ''Father?''
The carpenter said, ''Pinocchio?''

Kin Vassy
NASHVILLE, TENNESSEE

URTROOM

"That's All Right, I Trust You Anyhow":

POLITICIANS AND LAWYERS

Even So

Back in the old days a farmer drove his wagon into Frankfort, Kentucky, to do some trading. He stopped in front of a feed store but the store had no hitching post. Seeing a man standing nearby doing nothing, he asked, "Would you mind holding my team while I do some trading?"

"I'll have you know that I am a member of the legislature," the man said stiffly.

"That's all right," said the farmer, "I trust you anyhow."

Loyal Jones

Too Many Candidates

In many counties, the main people who ran for office were those who couldn't make a living otherwise, so you would always have several candidates who had physical handicaps. My father in Knott County told this story about all of the candidates for jailer being lined up on a jolt wagon ready to make speeches when one of them saw a dog coming down the street running on three legs. He turned to the other candidates and said, "Uh-oh, here comes another candidate for jailer."

Paul Wattles
BEREA, KENTUCKY

Up to Here

A senator was known to hit the bottle regularly, and sometimes he drank so much that he got sick. Once he and his opponent were speaking from the same platform. It was a hot day, the senator was pretty far gone, and halfway through his opponent's speech he ran to the side of the platform and threw up vigorously. He was a politician to the core, however, and he observed as he returned to his seat, "Every time I hear this man open his mouth, I get sick to my stomach!"

Loyal Jones

Taking No Chances

A politician was going up and down the roads campaigning when he saw a beautiful young woman milking a cow. He stopped to talk and politick for a while. Soon the girl's mother called from the house, "Who are you talking to?"

"Oh, just a politician," the young woman answered.

"You get yourself into this house this minute," the old woman yelled back. "And bring the cow with you."

Judge Ernie Wood
SOMERSET, KENTUCKY

Signs of the Times

One year when I was in eastern Kentucky along toward election time, I saw a series of white stakes driven at intervals alongside the road, but they were so far away that I couldn't figure out what they were. Actually they bore little signs advertising the merits of some enterprising candidate. I approached someone on the street, pointed to the stakes, and asked, "What do those mean?"

The man shook his head and said, "We won't know until after the election."

Dr. Thomas D. Clark
LEXINGTON, KENTUCKY

Two from Al

A Kentuckian got a job in Washington and moved there. After a few weeks, he wrote home, "I've got this place figured out. It's just one big Kentucky courthouse."

My kinfolks thought that electricity was invented by Franklin Delano Roosevelt.

Al Smith
LEXINGTON, KENTUCKY

Big Crowds

Down in the heavily Republican Fifth District of Kentucky, a man was bragging about going somewhere to hear a speech by his favorite, Dwight D. Eisenhower. "Why, there were ten thousand people there to hear that speech," he said.

"That's nothing," said a disgruntled Democrat. "When Hoover was president, I saw that many chasing a rabbit!"

Loyal Jones

Nary-Un

I heard Democratic Governor Bert T. Combs tell this joke on himself when he was governor. He was traveling in a Republican district of southeast Kentucky in a chauffeur-driven limousine. On seeing a little boy, not too well-dressed, sitting beside the road, he had the chauffeur stop the car, and he went over to the little boy with his hand outstretched and asked, "Sonny, do you know who your governor is?"

"Pa says we ain't got nary-un," the boy replied.

Paul Graham
EVARTS, KENTUCKY

Would I Lie?

Governor (later Senator) Bob Taylor of Tennessee was returning home late after a night out with the boys, tiptoeing, carrying his shoes, hoping not to awaken his wife. She woke and inquired what time it was. "About midnight," he replied.

Just then the clock struck three. "Did that clock strike three?" she asked.

"Are you going to believe a little old three-dollar clock or the governor of Tennessee?" he asked in an aggrieved tone.

Dr. Jim W. Miller
BOWLING GREEN, KENTUCKY

Possum on the Line

A lot of politicians brag about taking the middle of the road. All I've ever found in the middle of the road is a yellow line and dead possums.

Dr. Grady Stumbo
HINDMAN, KENTUCKY

There Is a Difference

A liberal and a conservative got to arguing over the difference between their philosophies. The liberal said, "If a man was fifty feet out in the lake drowning, a conservative would throw him a twenty-five foot rope and expect him to help himself by swimming halfway to the shore."

"And," said the conservative, "a liberal would throw the man a fifty-foot rope, but before he got him pulled to shore he would drop the rope and run off to do more good deeds."

Buddy Westbrook
LONDON, KENTUCKY

Universal Suffrage

It was election time, and two party men were out in the graveyard getting names off tombstones to put on absentee ballots. They came to an old stone that had so much moss on it, they had trouble reading the name of the deceased. "Let's just skip this one," said one of the men.

"No," said the other, "he's got just as much right to vote as anybody in the graveyard."

Nancy Jones
BEREA, KENTUCKY

-Isms

This is the way I've got it all figured out:

Socialism is when you have two cows and you have to give one to your neighbor

Communism is when you have two cows, the government takes both of them and gives you the milk

New Dealism is when you have two cows and the government takes both, shoots one, milks the other and throws the milk away

Nazism is when you have two cows, the government takes both and shoots you

Capitalism is when you have two cows, you sell one and buy a bull.

"Old Joe" Clark
BEREA, KENTUCKY

Incrimination

One time they called a character witness to the stand down in the North Carolina court presided over by a good friend of mine, Judge Harlin Johnston. The lawyer asked the witness, "Are you a member of the state legislature?"

Judge Johnston said, "What are you trying to do, impeach your own witness?"

Sen. Sam J. Ervin, Jr.
MORGANTON, NORTH CAROLINA

Some Have No Shame

Judge Patton was a famous eastern Kentucky judge who did not hesitate to give his opinion of wrongdoers. Once he was sitting in a circuit court in a county seat where they had built a new courthouse and had planted new trees all around it. In those days people came to town on court days to loaf, gossip, and trade horses, mules, and dogs. Men would tie their horses and mules to the new trees, and they had stripped off all of the leaves and gnawed the bark, killing the trees. He ordered the sheriff to round up the traders and loafers and to bring them into court. He gave them a stiff lecture and ended with these words: "There are people who would ride Balaam's ass into the city of Jerusalem and hitch him to the tree of life!"

Another story told on Judge Patton was about how he lectured a group of law enforcement officials on one particular type of character one might see in eastern Kentucky. "If you see a man sitting down at the forks of the road with a blue serge suit on and one of these little bowties on and a banjo fernenst* his breast, arrest that man, gentlemen, arrest him, for if he ain't done something, he's a-going to!"

Dr. Josiah Combs
KNOTT COUNTY, KENTUCKY

Good Price

A mountain county judge years ago was illiterate, but he could read figures, and so he kept a Sears-Roebuck catalogue on his desk to help him with setting fines. He found a man guilty of some minor offense, looked in his catalogue for a while, and then fined him $8.98. The miscreant protested, but his lawyer said, "Don't object. Be glad he was looking under pants rather than pianos."

Dr. Francis S. Hutchins
BEREA, KENTUCKY

Clearcut Decisions

The old judge was being interviewed by the local newspaperman. "How do you reach your decisions?" the newsman asked.

"Well, I listen to the plaintiff, and then I make my decision."

---

*across (Old English preposition; also means *opposite* or *next to*.)

"Don't you listen to the defense before you make up your mind?"

"No, I used to, but I found out that it just confused me."

Loyal Jones

High Advice

A man had some legal problems and went to a lawyer for help. The lawyer said, "You can ask me two questions for five hundred dollars."

"Isn't that kind of high?" the man asked.

"Yes," said the lawyer. "What's your second question?"

Judge Ernie Wood
SOMERSET, KENTUCKY

Hard Witness

A man came into a lawyer's office and said he wanted the lawyer to defend him on a charge of shooting a man. "Did you kill him?" the lawyer asked.

"No, he got well," the man answered.

"Well, I'll take your case," the lawyer said, "but he's going to be a mighty hard witness against you."

Loyal Jones

Running Out of Space

A man and his wife were strolling through a cemetery reading the epitaphs on the tombstones when they came to one that read, *A Lawyer and an Honest Man.*

"Well," said the man, "they must be getting crowded if they have to put two in the same grave."

Dr. Charles Harris
BEREA, KENTUCKY

Wham!

A lawsuit ensued after a head-on collision of two cars. The farmer who witnessed the wreck from his front porch was called to testify. "In your opinion," the lawyer for one of the drivers asked, "which of the drivers was at fault?" The farmer reflected for a while and answered, "Well, it seemed to me that they hit each other at about the same time.''

Loyal Jones

Convincing

Over around Waynesville, North Carolina, some years back, a fellow had gone off to the University of North Carolina Law School, graduated very high in his class, and could have gone to some other place and made a big-time lawyer, but he decided to come back home and help out the folks where he was raised. He had picked up a touch of that old bleeding-heart liberalism somewhere along the way, and he was always favoring the downtrodden classes, the underdogs. So when he was setting up his practice, he wanted to be sure that the poor folks around there knew he was there to help them. The first indigent person he heard about getting in trouble, he jumped right in there and took the case for nothing. His client was a little old man, up in years, who had been accused of stealing chickens from his neighbor's henhouse. They went to court, and the lawyer did everything he could to get the old man off. He was eloquent in arguing the man's innocence, a credit to a law school known for great lawyers. The man was found not guilty, and the lawyer took him across the street to a cafe and bought him some lunch. ''I took your case,'' he said, ''didn't charge you anything, so between you and me, I'd like to know if you did it or not?''

''Well,'' the old man said, ''when we commenced in there, I was of the opinion that I probably did it, but after I heard you talk, I don't believe I was anywhere around that man's chickenhouse.''

Jan Davidson
CULLOWHEE, NORTH CAROLINA

Reluctant Bedmate

An east Indian, a Jew, and a lawyer were traveling through the mountains when night overcame them. They decided to

stop at a farmer's house to ask if they could spend the night. The farmer agreed but said, "One of you will have to sleep in the barn since we have only two beds."

The Indian said that since he came from an undeveloped nation that he would be glad to sleep in the barn. He departed for the barn, but soon there came a knock at the door and the Indian was there, explaining, "There are cattle in the barn and since I believe that cattle are sacred, I don't feel that I should sleep in the barn."

The Jew said he did not mind sleeping in the barn, and he went out. Soon, however, he was back, saying, "There are pigs in the barn, and since we Jews feel that pigs are unclean, I don't think that I should sleep with them."

The lawyer said that in that case he would be glad to sleep in the barn. He left, and in about ten minutes there was another knock at the door. The farmer opened the door, and there stood the cows and the pigs.

Judge Ernie Woods
SOMERSET, KENTUCKY

Home Free

Another fellow, arrested for stealing a chicken, asked for a public defender, and a young fellow right out of law school was sent down to the jail to see him. He questioned him at length about his innocence, was convinced of it, and took the case. The young lawyer was quite an orator, and he prepared mightily for the case. He defended the alleged thief in the face of two eyewitnesses, and his summation before the jury was so eloquent and heart-rending that the jury took pity on the defendant and pronounced him not guilty. The lawyer walked out of court with the freed man, feeling proud that he had seen justice done. When they reached the street, the defendant asked, "Does this mean that I get to keep the chicken?"

Loyal Jones

Tactics

A young lawyer went to an old lawyer for advice as to how to try a lawsuit. The old lawyer said, "If the evidence is against you, talk about the law. If the law is against you, talk about the evidence."

The young lawyer said, "But what do you do when both the evidence and the law are against you?"

"In that event," said the old lawyer, "give somebody hell. That will distract the attention of the judge and the jury from the weakness of the case."

Sen. Sam J. Ervin, Jr.
MORGANTON, NORTH CAROLINA

Damn the Law

The old justice of the peace was exasperated by the tactics of the young lawyer trying his first case. The young lawyer kept rising and exclaiming, "I object. You are not proceeding according to law."

Finally the old magistrate could stand it no longer. He shouted, "Young man, quit jumping up and saying, 'I object. You are not proceeding according to law.' I'll have you understand I am running this court. The law hasn't got a damn thing to do with it."

Sen. Sam J. Ervin, Jr.

Never Felt Better

Jake Sizemore and his wife Sally decided to hook up their old horse and buggy and take a little sashay into town. They put their dog Buford in the seat between them, clucked "Gitty-up there, Duchess!" at the horse, and headed out their farm road that led to the main highway.

Just as they turned north on Highway 25E here come a red Porsche over the hill in the wrong lane, headed south to Knoxville, and it crashed into the horse and knocked it back amongst the buggy full of Jake, Sally, and Buford, who went flying into the air along with wheels, surrey fringes, picnic baskets, buggy springs, and horsehair, landing in and around the highway ditch, part of them, and the rest of them scattered all over Red Lane's hayfield. It was an awful crash. It was a miracle, too, that anybody survived it.

A couple of weeks later Jake's back kept acting up on him, so he talked it over with Sally and she said she thought they ought to sue the driver of the red Porsche for damages, physical and mental.

When it got to court the defendant's Knoxville lawyer was working hard to discredit Jake. He was aggressive and pushy and, thinking he had Jake in a corner, smiled an insinuating, obnoxious smile (reminded Jake of a possum eating persimmons) and said, "Now, sir, we have your statement on record, taken at the scene of the accident, in which you declared your condition to be fine. In fact, the state trooper wrote down your exact words. He said you said you'd never felt better. And yet, several weeks later, you suddenly decide that you don't feel so good. Would you care to tell us why you've changed your story?"

"Well, sir," Jake said, "when I come to, after that Porsche hit us, I seen my dog Buford laying in the ditch. When the officer walked over to him, Buford barked at him. So the officer pulled out his gun and shot him. Then the officer walked over to my horse, Duchess, and she kicked at him, so he shot her too. Then he walked straight to me, the gun still in his hand with the barrel smoking, looked at me sour-like, and said, 'And how do you feel?'

"I told him I never felt better in my life!"

Billy Edd Wheeler
and Chet Atkins
NASHVILLE, TENNESSEE

St. Peter's Lawsuit

St. Peter was out walking along the wall that separates heaven and hell one day and he noticed that the wall was getting shabby in places. There was one bad spot in particular where several bricks had fallen out, so St. Peter called Lucifer on the phone to complain. He said, "Now look here, you're going to have to do something about your side of the wall. It's starting to look pretty bad." When Lucifer heard who it was, he just hung up.

A couple weeks later St. Peter was out touring the wall again and noticed that the bad spot had gotten worse. So many bricks had fallen out and the concrete was so crumbly a small hole was starting to develop. It bothered St. Peter so much he called Lucifer immediately and started giving him the devil about the wall, but once again as soon as Lucifer recognized the voice, he hung up.

The third time St. Peter called he said, "Now listen, Lucifer, don't you hang up. That wall is a disgrace. There's a hole in it almost big enough for somebody to crawl through, and it's time you lived up to your part of the bargain and fixed it. If you don't fix it and start maintaining it properly, well, I have no choice: I'll have to sue you."

"That's fine," Lucifer said, chuckling, "but tell me something, Pete, old boy. Where are you going to get your lawyers?"

Mary Charlotte McCall
TALLAHASSEE, FLORIDA

Lawyers Replace White Mice

Several scientific journals have noted a new trend in the research community of the United States: white mice are being replaced by lawyers for experimental purposes.

The reasons for this phenomenon are three:

1. There's more of them.
2. You gotta admit they're smarter than you are.
3. You don't get all that attached to them.

Mary Charlotte McCall

''Just Show Him Your Badge'':

MOUNTAINEERS AND THE LAW

The Bull and the Badge

One day these old boys were down at the barn doing some farm work, and they heard some shots. They looked up and here coming through the field was a big old long, tall boy—his legs ran all the way to his shoulders—he was running low down—Buckshot was his nickname. He was the local bootlegger. The sheriff was after him. That was who was doing the shooting.

Buckshot ran into the barn and yelled, ''Where can I hide? The sheriff's after me!''

The other two said, ''Get in the stall and we'll tell the sheriff we haven't seen you.''

He jumped into the stall and proceeded to climb over a seven-foot wall, thinking he would get out and run away. But as soon as his feet hit the ground they heard him squalling. He had jumped down into a lot with the meanest Jersey bull you've ever seen. They ran to the door and there was Buckshot running through the field with the Jersey bull right behind him, and when he got to the other side, he cleared a six-foot fence and never touched a wire.

About that time the sheriff came into the barn and said, "Have you seen Buckshot?"

They said, "No, we haven't seen him. Anyway, this is private property, what are you doing here?"

He stuck his badge out and said, "This *badge* says I can look for him anyplace in this county!"

They said, "Well, he lit out through the field and over the hill there." They pointed toward the bull lot. The sheriff took out that way and didn't see the bull. But the bull saw him and took out after him. He started running back toward the barn, yelling, "Open the door and let me in!"

One of the old boys stuck his head out through the door and hollered, "Oh, just show him your *badge!*"

Dr. Carl Hurley
LEXINGTON, KENTUCKY

Planting Time

The sheriff thought Ike Vance was pretty dumb to write a letter like he did to his wife from Moundsville where he was serving time in the penitentiary on charges of robbing the Slab Fork Lumber Company office and making away with several thousand dollars in cold cash, which he buried in tin cans somewhere but nobody knew exactly where. The letter said in part, "Whatever you do don't dig up the garden this year. Wait till I tell you when."

This was plenty for the warden.

He called the sheriff and the sheriff sent a posse of men out and they dug that garden from one end to the other. When Ike heard about it, he wrote to his wife, "Go ahead now, honey, and plant the garden."

Jim Comstock, Editor
The West Virginia Hillbilly
RICHWOOD, WEST VIRGINIA

Hard To Do Some People a Favor

Down in north Georgia some people lived on this long dirt road back off the main road, and some of the boys got to going over there on Saturday night and drag-racing. This upset the residents, and one of them, who was politically connected, called the governor and asked him to do something to catch the racers. So the governor called up the director of the state police and asked him to send a patrolman to investigate. He sent a young cop from around Atlanta.

Now the young cop was a little nervous because he had heard tales about the mountaineers, but he went on up there and started driving down that long dirt road waving cordially at all of the folks sitting on their front porches. He drove along to where a great big old boy was standing by the road just before a big curve. The cop waved and grinned and said howdy to the young man, who reared back and yelled at the top of his lungs, ''Pig!'' Well, this made the policeman so mad that he gunned his cruiser and went sliding around this curve, throwing dirt every which way, and he ran into a four-hundred-pound Duroc-Jersey hog; tore up his cruiser and killed that hog.

Loyal Jones

The Circle Fly

A Kentucky mountain farmer decided to go to town one day, and he came onto the interstate, nearly colliding with a state patrol cruiser. The policeman pulled him over, started talking to him, said, ''Didn't you see that yield sign back there?''

''Yes,'' he said, ''and I yield as loud as I could.''

The policeman thought, ''Well, this old hillbilly—I'll just let him go.''

The farmer went on down the road and had a flat tire. He pulled off the road and was working on his tire, and the same policeman came by. He hadn't got off the road far enough—didn't suit the policeman. He said, "Old man, I'll have to write you a ticket." Then he said, "By the way, what's that goldenrod doing on the back of your truck and that columbine on the front?"

The farmer said, "Well, when I took my driving test, they said if anything happened to my truck, that I was supposed to put flares in front and back, and that's what I done."

The policeman said, "I let you by before, but you're a smart-aleck, and I'm going to write you up a ticket." So he was writing up a ticket, and there was a fly that kept flying around his face, and he kept swatting at it, and the old farmer just stood there watching him.

He said, "That's a circle fly." The policeman didn't pay any attention, just kept on writing the ticket. The farmer said again, "That's a circle fly."

Finally the policeman said, "All right. What is a circle fly?"

The farmer said, "Down where I live, we work down in the bottoms along the river where the humidity is sort of high and it's hot down there, and when you're plowing, these flies will just circle around the horse's rear end."

That made the policeman real indignant, and he said, "Are you calling me a horse's ass?"

The farmer said, "No, but you can't hardly fool a circle fly."

Charles Tribble
CYNTHIANA, KENTUCKY

Somebody Was At Fault

A farmer pulled his hay wagon out into the Blowing Rock Road in front of a tourist who came tearing down the road not looking where he was going. He hit the wagon and did a lot of damage to his car. He jumped out, hot under the collar, all jacked out of shape, and said, "Look what you've done to my car!"

The farmer said, "Well, I'm sorry. I know it was my fault, but the law will be along in a few minutes, so just sit back and cool off. Don't get nervous or you'll bust a gut. Here, have a drink of liquor while we wait."

So the guy accepted, and he began to cool off with every swallow he'd take. After a while the law arrived and the farmer said, "Why, this S.O.B. was drunk, and he ran right into me!"

William E. Lightfoot
BOONE, NORTH CAROLINA

Real Ugly

Down in North Carolina there was a family named Johnson who lived way back in the mountains. One Saturday night, two of the Johnson boys, Jake and Luke, went out riding in a flatbed truck, looking for some fun or adventure. "I'll tell you what," Jake said to Luke. "I been wanting some fresh meat. Let's go down to Old Man Phillips's place and steal one of his Chester White hogs."

So they drove over beside the man's hog lot, got out and hemmed a big shoat, caught it, and brought it back to the truck. Since they had no sideboards or tailgate on the truck, they had a problem, but Jake solved it by putting the hog in between them on the front seat. After some squealing and struggling, it settled down, and they took off. However, when they got to the main road, heading home, they saw the sheriff's cruiser sitting by the road.

"Uh-oh," said Jake, "I bet he follows us."

Sure enough, the sheriff took after them with his light on and siren at full blast. Jake pulled over, took off his coat and threw it around the hog and put his hat on its head. The sheriff came up beside the window, shined his light on Jake and asked, "What's your name, boy?"

"I'm Jake Johnson, Sheriff, and that's my brother Luke over there." The sheriff shined his light on Luke and then pointed it at the hog, which was sitting quietly, looking straight ahead.

"What's your name?" the sheriff asked.

Jake rammed the hog in the ribs with his elbow, and it went, "Oink."

The sheriff stepped back and said, "You boys go on now

and don't get into no trouble, y'hear?''

Jake said, ''Yes, sir,'' and took off.

The sheriff went back to his cruiser, shaking his head. He got in and said to his deputy, ''You know, I've been sheriff of this county for twenty years, and I thought I'd seen everything, but damned if that Oink Johnson ain't the ugliest rascal I ever laid eyes on!''

Loyal Jones

Wanted Men Captured

The FBI sent out a bulletin to all police chiefs and sheriffs all over the country along with a picture of a dangerous criminal they hoped to capture. The picture showed the criminal from three angles, the front and left and right profiles.

Within a few hours the FBI received a telegram from a county sheriff deep in Appalachia. It read: ''I got your photographs and am happy to report that I have captured all three men.''

Billy Edd Wheeler

A Miracle

A moonshiner had hidden his wares in an outbuilding. One day the revenue officers came and searched until they found the jugs. As they unscrewed the caps to smell the contents, the moonshiner prayed to be delivered from what looked like sure incrimination. After smelling all of the jugs, one of the revenuers said, ''Why, there's nothing but water in these jugs.''

''Hit's a miracle,'' the moonshiner exclaimed.

Harry M. Caudill
WHITESBURG, KENTUCKY

Fishing with Coffee and Biscuits

This fellow, Quill, he lived way back in the woods and he hunted and fished all the time, and didn't pay any attention to the hunting seasons or laws or anything, and he knew the woods better than the game warden.

The game warden had been trying to catch Quill for a long time. Today he knew the sign was right—he knew Quill would be up early to go fishing. So he snuck down there in the middle of the night and hid up on top of Quill's house. This way he knew he had the jump on Quill. He'd let him head out and then he'd follow him, be right on his trail, hide in the woods until Quill had caught a large, illegal bunch of fish, and he'd catch him.

As it started to get a little bit of daylight, he could hear Quill get up, start a fire, and put the coffee on. His stomach started growling at the smell of that coffee and those fresh-smelling biscuits as they baked in the oven. He could hardly contain himself, when out walked Quill on the porch and hollered, "Come on down here and git some of this coffee and biscuits while they're hot! I know you're out there!" He went back in and shut the door.

The game warden could not believe it. He climbed down and walked up on the porch and into the house and exclaimed, "Well, how did you know I was out there?"

Quill said, "I didn't. I walk out there and say that ever morning, just in case ye are!"

Fred Park
BEREA, KENTUCKY

"There's More to Farming Than Sex":

ANIMALS AND HUNTING

Bull

A man was driving down the road when he saw a man trying to plow with a big bull. The bull was snorting and kicking, balking and trying to run, and the farmer hadn't done more than scratch a crooked track in the field. The man pulled over to watch, and then he saw a new John Deere tractor standing in a shed nearby. His curiosity got the best of him, and he called to the farmer, "How come you're plowing that bull when you have a new tractor up there in the shed?"

"I'm trying to teach this consarned bull that there's more to farming than sex."

Loyal Jones

Bill

A tourist stopped to admire a North Carolina mule. He asked the mule's owner what the animal's name was. The farmer replied, "I don't know, but we call it Bill."

Sen. Sam J. Ervin, Jr.
MORGANTON, NORTH CAROLINA

Curing the Cross-Eyed Mule

A young farmer in the Berea, Kentucky, area always dreamed of owning a fine steep-faced blue-nosed mule, and after several years of scrimping and saving he was able to acquire one in a hardship sale. Got a beauty, a young mule with a light blue coat, dark ears, and a perfect conformation.

He couldn't wait to show off his mule, so one Sunday afternoon he invited all his neighbors over and had them wait at the house while he went down to the barn to hitch up the mule to a big sled with wooden runners. He loaded the sled with heavy tools and implements, barrels of feed, sacks of fertilizer, and topped it off with several bales of hay.

"Git up!" he clucked, and the mule strained in its harness, finally got started up the steep hill as the man beamed with pride. About halfway to the house the sled got stuck in a drainage ditch and the mule couldn't go forward, just pulled and strained, pulled and strained, as the farmer urged him on, but to no avail. The mule gave one final pull, snorted, his eyes crossed, and he dropped flat on his belly to the ground.

The farmer worked himself into a tizzy pulling at the mule, yelling at him, slapping him on the flanks, but he couldn't get the mule up. His pride turned to consternation, frustration, irritation, then to concern. Finally in desperation he called the local veterinarian.

The vet arrived in his black suit and black hat, studied the situation, knelt in front of the mule, lifted the mule's head, and looked into its crossed eyes. And, holding one jaw gently in his left hand, whacked across the other jaw with the edge of his right hand. The mule's eyes clicked and uncrossed. Then the vet took an eighteen-inch section of black hose from his large black bag, inserted part of it into the mule's rear end, took a deep breath, blew a sharp *whoof!* into the hose, and, lo, the mule rose to its feet. The farmer smiled in amazement, relieved.

"That'll be fifteen dollars," the vet said, and the farmer paid it gladly. "But now remember, this is a young mule. He's not full-strength mature yet, so you break him in slow and don't go overloading him. If this happens again we might not be able to fix it."

As soon as the vet was gone the farmer unloaded the sled of about half of its cargo, decided to let the mule pull the smaller load on up to the house. But he'd bragged so much about his new mule he just didn't want to pull up there with such a small load, so he added a few things back on. Then a few more things. Pretty soon the sled was almost as full as before. "Git up!" he clucked, and the sled inched its way on up the hill. Pretty soon, though, the mule came to a stop. Strained. Then its eyes crossed and it dropped again in its tracks.

Now the farmer was really beside himself. People were waiting to see his fine new mule. What was he to do? Well, he didn't want to call the vet and spend another fifteen dollars. He ran to the barn, chopped off a section of garden hose, came back, and, just as he'd seen the vet do, inserted one end of it into the mule's rear end. He blew into the hose, he whoofed, he huffed and puffed until he was blue in the face, but the mule didn't rise. Finally he called the vet back.

The vet saw the hose sticking out of the mule, shook his head disapprovingly at the young farmer, knelt in front of the mule, lifted its head and looked into its eyes, gave it a precise whack across the jaw as before, and the mule's eyes clicked and uncrossed.

Then he took the garden hose out of the mule, turned it around, gave one sharp *whoof!* of a blow, and the mule rose once again to its feet.

"I don't know how you do that," the farmer said, "but here's your money, and I'm much obliged. But, if you don't mind me asking, how come you turned that hose around before you blew into it?"

The vet replied with a disdainful scowl, "You don't think I'd put the same end in *my* mouth that you'd had in yours, do you?"

Bruce Fraley
BEREA, KENTUCKY

Curing a Mule of the Bots

A farmer came to his neighbor's house one time and asked him, "Ambrose, didn't you have a mule come down sick with the bots one time?"

"Yep."

"Well, what did you do for it?"

"Fed him turpentine."

"Hmm, thank you," the farmer said and went back home, shaking his head in wonder.

A few weeks later the farmer returned, said, "Ambrose, what did you say you gave your mule for the bots?"

"Turpentine."

"Hmm, that's what I thought you said. Well, by golly, I fed mine some turpentine—and it killed him!"

"Yep," Ambrose said drily. "Killed mine too."

Billy Edd Wheeler

Mule Maintenance

A fellow was driving his mule and wagon down the road, and a tourist came flying by in his car and ran into the mule, hurt it badly. He got out and said, "Gosh, did I hurt your mule?"

The farmer said, "Well, if you think you done him any good, I'd be happy to pay you fer it."

William E. Lightfoot
BOONE, NORTH CAROLINA

Mortgage on the Hogs

Alec Burnett lived up there on Mill Creek in North Carolina. He was a waggish sort of fellow and had a habit of drinking. He had fun wherever he went. He had been down at Old Fort and bought a cow. He'd gotten ahold of some booze somewhere along the line, and he had a little pistol. It occurred to him that it would be fun to run the cow through Old Fort and fire off the pistol. He did it, and they hailed him before the magistrate and fined him ten dollars and the cost. "Well," he said. "I don't have a cent of money."

"We can secure the cow," the magistrate said.

"The cow's not mine," answered Alec.

"Well, have you got something else?"

"Well, I've got some hogs and an old army rifle, the kind used in the War Between the States."

"How many hogs do you have?"

"Well, five or six; we'll say five."

"Well, we'll take a mortgage on the hogs, and you can pay it when you can. If you can't pay it or won't pay it, we'll come and get the hogs." So he gave a mortgage on five bay hogs with brown noses and short tails. In the fullness of time he defaulted on the payment. So one morning an officer, a deputy, came up to Mill Creek at his home to get the hogs. He says, "They're up the hollow here." They started on up there, and he passed around the chimney corner and picked up a mattock. He put it on his shoulder and they walked up Mill Creek, and he said, "You'll have to be quiet. Them hogs are pretty wild."

"They're not all that wild, are they?" the deputy asked.

"Oh," he said, "yes, they're pretty wild. I guess you knowed they was groundhogs, didn't you?"

"Well," said the deputy, "what about the gun?"

"The gun?" he said, "I left that at Seven Pines.* I set it down agin a tree and run, but you can have it if you want to go get it."

Bascom Lamar Lunsford
LEICESTER, NORTH CAROLINA

The Cat Contingent

This lady had a great big old black Persian cat, and it got sick. She tried everything she could think of to cure it, but it didn't seem to do any good, so she decided to call the vet. "My cat's sick. What can I do?"

The vet thought she said "cow," so he said the best thing

---

*A Civil War battle.

to do was give it about a quart of castor oil.

She said, "Isn't that too much?"

He said, "No, it's about the right amount." So she got her cat and poured about a quart of castor oil down its throat.

Well, the cat disappeared. She looked everywhere for it, but she couldn't find it. Then she asked all the neighbors if they had seen it. Finally one said yes, she believed she had seen it recently, in the company of about six other cats.

The owner said, "That surprises me, for mine is a very sick cat. What were they doing?"

The neighbor said, "Well, two of them were digging holes, two were covering up, and two were scouting for new territory!"

Loyal Jones

A Dog in Heat

A man was sitting on a park bench reading his paper when this stray dog ran up and became quite familiar. He stood up and grabbed the man's knee with his forepaws and started humping amorously against the man's leg.

The man was embarrassed, as people were watching, so he tried to shoo the dog away with his paper. But the dog ignored him and continued to make love to his leg. The man got mad, looked the dog in the eyes, and said in his gruffest voice, "Cut that out!"

The dog's eyes turned evil and he emitted a mean, low, gutteral, teeth-displaying "GR-RR-RRRROO-O-OOOOW-WLL!"

The man smiled at the dog and in a very pacifying tone said, "Well . . . hurry up, then."

Chet Atkins
NASHVILLE, TENNESSEE

Bad Luck

The county agricultural agent came out to visit a backwoods farmer. They talked for a while, and then he asked, "How's your poultry doing?"

"Oh, no good," the farmer answered. "We planted two

rows but the chickens scratched it up."

Max Woody
OLD FORT, NORTH CAROLINA

Adjustments

"Joe, what were you doing with that billy goat this evening?"

"I thought it might rain tonight, and he's like myself, he couldn't take another weather warping."

"Were you putting him in the barn?"

"No, I ain't got no barn. I took and put him in my bedroom. I tied him to the head of my bed."

"You keep him in your bedroom?"

"He's right there in my bedroom."

"What about the smell?"

"He'll just have to get used to it."

"Old Joe" Clark
BEREA, KENTUCKY

Generous Pig

I was going through the country and got lost, so I stopped for directions at a house where there was a lady on the porch, and some young'uns running around, and a pet pig in the yard. I got my directions and asked for some water, since I was pretty thirsty. The lady said she had just churned and asked whether I wanted some fresh buttermilk. "That'd be fine," I said. So she brought me a nice cool bowl of buttermilk and I turned it up and drunk it. The pig came over and went to rubbing about my legs as I drank from the bowl. I said, "That's a friendly pig. How come?"

The lady said, "You're drinking your buttermilk out of his bowl."

Glenn Baker
FAIRMONT, WEST VIRGINIA

Salty

This is the first joke I ever heard my mother tell. Back in the old days when people were riding buses from one town to the other, they'd have boxes with strings and ropes around them on the baggage racks above the seats. If they were traveling a long ways, they'd take picnic baskets. The men who rode the buses would look up there and see where the picnic baskets were, so they might get a free meal. This man got on the bus, saw a basket up on the rack and sat down under it by a lady. They were riding along, and he felt something dripping across his face. He licked his lips and asked, "Pickles, ma'am?"

She turned to him and said, "No, pups."

Billy Wilson
BEREA, KENTUCKY

He's Not Talking Now

A man went into a pet shop and bought himself a talking parrot. About a week later, he went back to the shop and told the salesman that the bird had quit talking. The fellow said, "Well, I think I know the problem. The top part of the beak there tends to get too long, and it's hard for the parrot to work it then. Take him home and file it off a little and he'll be able to start talking again."

About three weeks later the bird's owner was coming down the street by the pet shop, and the salesman saw him and ran out and said, "How's that parrot?"

He said, "It's dead!"

"Oh, no, what happened? Did you file the beak back too far, so that it couldn't eat?"

The old boy said, "Naw, I think he was dead when I took his head out of the vice."

Dr. Carl Hurley
LEXINGTON, KENTUCKY

Where's Noah When You Need Him?

Rich and Tom went to town and bought this animal of the four-legged variety, dark grey, with long ears. Well, it was a hot day and as they were walking along, all of a sudden this animal gives a big loud "Heeee-haaww" and falls over dead.

Well, on hot days you have to do something about dead

animals or they'll get to smelling bad, and so the two boys started thinking about digging a hole and what they would put on the headstone. They disagreed on what kind of animal he was, as Tom thought he was a donkey and Rich said it was a burro. Finally they saw Preacher Brown coming down the road, so they asked him. He closed his eyes and thought about it awhile, and then opened his eyes and opened his Bible and said, "Now, boys, the Good Book says that this animal is an ass."

So now they both knew what it was, and they thanked the preacher, who went on his way, and they started to dig the grave.

Down the road comes Johnny Jones, a seven-year-old, very curious, friendly little guy, and he says, "Howdy, boys, whatcha doing, digging a foxhole?"

Tom said, "Not according to Preacher Brown."

Pamela Sue Hunt
RICHMOND, KENTUCKY

The Unmistakable Cat

This old boy was coming out of the woods after cutting pulpwood. Driving through town in his big two-ton truck, he got right in front of the vet's office and ran over a cat. He was upset, so he ran into the doctor's office saying, "Doc, get out here as quick as you can, I think I've run over one of the cats from your clinic that must have got loose!"

The veterinarian asked, "What's it look like?"

The truck driver said, "It's about that thin, and about that long . . ."

Dr. Carl Hurley
LEXINGTON, KENTUCKY

Heavy Subject

An old fellow passed a schoolhouse where a boy was coming out from school. He was driving a little horse on the offside (skinny). Just as he got even with the boy, he popped his whip and said, "Get up, Heavy."

The boy said, "It don't look to me like he's much heavy."

The old man said, "Well, if you had lifted him up as many times as I have, you would think he was heavy."

Bascom Lamar Lunsford
LEICESTER, NORTH CAROLINA

Proof

A farmer had three milk cows, and he had an unusually smart dog, Old Brownie, who would go get the cows for milking no matter where they were in a huge pasture. One day a cattle buyer came by and offered the farmer a high price for one of the cows, and so he sold her. At milking time that night, Old Brownie went for the cows and could only find the two. He brought them in and went back looking for the third, stayed out a long time, went out again and again. The farmer finally had to show Old Brownie the check for the cow before he would quit looking for her.

Russell Hensley
BEREA, KENTUCKY

Bullish

A man was walking down a rural road when he saw the mailman park his car and start across a pasture toward a farmhouse. When he got about halfway across, a huge Jersey bull flew out of a grove of trees after him. The mailman took off, his mailbag sailing along behind him, the bull gaining on him with every step. He and the bull got to the fence at the same time, and he threw himself over the fence, scattering his mail every which way. While he was picking up his mail the observer said, "He mighty nigh got you that time." The mailman looked up and said, "He mighty nigh gets me every time."

Loyal Jones

More Bull

A man asked a farmer if he could cross his pasture to catch the bus. The farmer replied, "You sure can, and if that old bull sees you, you may be able to beat the bus to wherever you're going."

Loyal Jones

It Depends

A stranger knocked on the door of a farmer and asked, "How much is that cow worth that is grazing down there alongside the road?"

"That depends," the farmer answered, "on whether you are the tax assessor or whether you just run over her with your car."

Loyal Jones

That's Horse Trading

Farmer Johnson was passing Farmer Smith's place one day, and he saw a horse he liked. He made an offer and bought it. Since Farmer Johnson was to be gone from home for a couple of days, Farmer Smith said he would have his boys deliver the horse in their truck. The boys went for the horse as instructed but rushed back to tell their dad that the horse was dead. He pondered the situation for a moment and then said, "Go pick up that dead horse and take it to Farmer Johnson's field."

Farmer Smith expected trouble from Farmer Johnson as soon as he returned home. For days, though, he heard nothing. Finally, he could stand it no longer, and he rode over to Farmer Johnson's place. After some casual conversation about crops and the weather, he inquired, "How is your horse doing?"

Farmer Johnson said, "Would you believe this? When I got home I found that horse dead out there in the field."

Farmer Smith said, "What? I'm sure sorry to hear that."

Farmer Johnson said, "Oh, there's no problem. I sold chances and raffled the horse off to get my money back, and I made a profit!"

"How in the world could you get by with raffling off a dead horse?" Farmer Smith asked.

Farmer Johnson said, "Nobody complained except the fellow who won. He raised so much hell I finally gave him back his dollar."

Paul Graham
BENHAM, KENTUCKY

Forewarned

Buyer: "That mule you sold me is almost blind!"

Seller: "Well, I told you before you bought him he didn't look good."

Billy Edd Wheeler

Willing Hogs

This farmer had a lot of sow hogs that needed to be bred, so one morning he loaded them all up in the truck and drove them to the farm where the farmer lived who owned the boars. After all the hogs had been bred the farmer asked the breeder, "How will I know if your boar hogs were successful?"

"Tomorrow morning look out your window. If your sows are out there eating grass, you'll know it 'took,' so don't worry. If they aren't eating grass, then it *didn't* take. Just load them up and bring them back and we'll have them bred again. No extra charge."

Next morning the farmer looked out the window. Not a single hog was eating grass. So he loaded them up and drove back to the breeder's farm and had them all bred again. Next morning the same thing—not one of those hogs was eating grass. He loaded them up and drove them back to be bred again. This went on for over a week, until he was getting tired of it.

On the seventh morning he didn't have the heart to look out the window, so he said to his wife, "Honey, if you don't mind, look out there and see if any of them hogs is eating grass."

"No," she said, "they ain't."

"What are they doing?"

"Well," she said, "they're all up in the truck except one, and she's in the front behind the steering wheel blowing the horn!"

Bobby David
NASHVILLE, TENNESSEE

The Unlucky Burglar

This man decided he'd take up burglary, so he got some tools and a flashlight and set out one dark night to try his hand at robbing houses. He found a nice house, jimmied the basement door open, and started climbing the stairs to the main part of the house. He turned a corner and froze when he heard a voice in the darkness say, "Jesus is watching you."

He shined his light and saw the gleaming green eyes of a Doberman. As he started to step cautiously away he heard the voice again: "Jesus is watching you."

It gave him a spooky feeling until he shined the light into the kitchen and saw a parrot sitting on a swing in a cage. The parrot said it again: "Jesus is watching you."

He walked over to the parrot and snapped, "Is that all you can say, you little green nitwit?"

"Sic him, Jesus!" the parrot said.

Chet Atkins
and Bobby Bare
NASHVILLE, TENNESSEE

The Parrot That Prayed

A nice respectable lady bought a parrot and brought it home, only to find that it cursed like a sailor. One of its favorite tricks was to sit in the corner and shout, "I'm a whore! I'm a whore!"

She was so embarrassed she didn't know what to do. The pet store had a policy of no-returns. Each sale was final. She couldn't give it away, for fear of having someone think the parrot learned to speak that way at her house. She was in a quandary. Finally she went to see her preacher about it.

"You're in luck," the preacher said. "I happen to have a parrot that is very religious. All he does is sit in the corner and pray. I tell you, that's the prayingest parrot you ever saw. Why don't we put your parrot in with mine and see if it doesn't tone her down, make her talk better. I have a feeling that my parrot will have a great influence on your parrot."

The lady agreed, brought her parrot to the preacher's house and, sure enough, there was his parrot sitting in the corner of the cage, his eyes closed, just praying up a storm. They opened the cage door, placed the lady's parrot inside, and she didn't waste any time. She hopped up on the swing and barked out, "I'm a whore! I'm a whore!"

The preacher's parrot stopped praying, opened his eyes, looked up and said, "It's a miracle. Thank God, my prayers have been answered!"

Billy Edd Wheeler

Getting Even

A man was standing on the corner in a small town waiting for the light to change when he noticed a blind man with a seeing-eye dog waiting beside him. The dog raised his leg and urinated on the leg of his master. The blind man reached in his pocket and started feeding the dog a cookie. Trying to be helpful the man spoke, "Are you aware that your dog is peeing on your leg?"

"Yes, I am," the blind man said, "and when I locate his head with this cookie, I'm going to kick him in the tail."

Loyal Jones

The Talking Dog

In 1901 I was with a medicine show, Dr. Rucker's Korak Wonder Company. Among other performers we had with us a ventriloquist by the name of Nobby Scales. Nobby could throw his voice farther than the champion hog-caller of Roane County, and when it lit there it stayed.

He was particularly clever at making animals appear to talk and was one of the big shots in the Korak Company. As usual, the show "blew" in Hannibal, Missouri, and Nobby and I were left there without a dime.

He said, "Wilson, I think I can get us some money. Go over there in that Dutchman's saloon and wait for me. And when I come in don't recognize me, but see that I don't get hurt."

I walked over, hung around the saloon stove a few

minutes, and in walked Nobby, followed by a little yellow cur dog. Walking up to the bar he ordered a drink of whiskey and turning to the dog he asked him what he would have. Lo and behold the dog piped back: "I'll take a ham sandwich!"

The bartender nearly fainted, as Nobby reached in the glass bowl and tossed the dog a sandwich which was hurriedly gobbled up. I could hardly keep my face straight as the saloon man looked at Nobby, then the dog, and then turned to look at his own visage in the mirror, to see if he was actually awake or just dreaming. The whiskey and sandwich gone, Nobby ordered another glass and then addressed the dog.

"What'll you have, Jack?" he asked. The dog looked up at him and said, "I'll take another ham sandwich."

The order was filled and by this time the Dutchman could stand it no longer. He leaped over the bar and fairly shouted at Nobby, "My God, man, do you mean to tell me that dog can *talk?*"

"Yes," said Nobby, "but I've about got him broke."

The bartering then started. The Dutchman wanted the dog and would pay a good price for him. After Mr. Scales had explained that this was the only talking dog in the world they struck a bargain. Nobby received five hundred dollars in cash and a ten-day note for five hundred dollars more. As he started to the door with his money he turned to the bartender and told him to tie the dog up or he would follow him out.

The Dutchman tied him to the icebox and just as Nobby reached the door, the dog (apparently) said: "So you sold me cause I could talk?"

Nobby says, "Yes, Jack—I sold you because you could talk."

"Well," replied the dog, "I'll never say another word until the Dutchman pays the note!"

Riley Wilson
CHARLESTON, WEST VIRGINIA

None of Your Beeswax

A man in Mitchell County, North Carolina, was working a yoke of oxen to a wagon when one of the oxen lay down and sulled up. It was a rough road and a hard pull, and the farmer wasn't able to get the ox to get up. So he unhooked the ox and put his head into the yoke. He and the other ox pulled the wagon on up the hill. When they reached the top, the ox started going faster and faster, first at a trot and then at a lope. Of course, the old man had to run to keep up. On the way home, they ran over a bee gum, and the bees started stinging them, and the ox ran faster. When they came into the barnyard, they knocked over a shed, causing a big commotion. As they went by the house, the old man yelled to his kinfolks sitting on the porch, "Here we come! Head us, damn our souls! Head us!"

Bascom Lamar Lunsford
LEICESTER, NORTH CAROLINA

More Oxen, More Stingers

An old farmer was very poor and had only a yoke of oxen to farm with, and during the winter, one of his oxen died. They didn't have money to buy another one, and when it came time to plow, the farmer said he'd yoke himself up to the plow with the ox and his wife could do the plowing. They started across the field doing pretty well until they plowed up a yellowjackets' nest. The yellowjackets started stinging the old man and the ox. The ox took off dragging the old man along with him. His wife came along behind them as fast as she could go. Eventually they hit a fence and got tangled up. The yellowjackets kept stinging them, and the ox bellowed and kicked. The old woman caught up with them and began trying to get the oxbow from around her husband's neck. In exasperation, he yelled, "Unhook the ox,' dammit! I'll stand!"

Dr. Boyd Carter
CLINTWOOD, VIRGINIA

Wide-Range Fishing

The Cullowhee Fire Department was having a benefit auction not long ago, and people donated things to sell. One of the things donated by a sporting goods store was a fish-attractor light, like you hang over the side of your boat, you know. Colonel Lusk was the auctioneer, he's a great salesman, he's reading right off the box, he says, "This light will attract bass. This light will attract trout, pike, crappy. This light will attract shrimp. By God, boys, you won't ever have to go to the beach again, if you get one of these!"

Jan Davidson
CULLOWHEE, NORTH CAROLINA

Ernie the Lion-Hearted

The Hunt Club was deep in Appalachia but it was in a fairly big city. This was a prestigious club, and not just anybody could belong to it. You had to have killed something ferocious, like a wild boar or a bear, to be asked to become a member, and you had to be well connected. It wasn't a place where good old boys talked about their hound dogs while swilling down Pabst Blue Ribbon beer. It was where rich old boys sipped rare Kentucky bourbon and talked about their hound dogs. Sometimes. Most of the time they talked about stalking big game.

Except Ernie McConnell. Ernie was a loner. He used to be quite gabby, they say, but that all changed gradually down through the years until now about all he did was sit in the corner and read *The Wall Street Journal.*

One evening after a fine dinner of rack-of-lamb some of the regulars were recounting their most memorable hunts, laughing and drinking toasts to various horn, fang, tusk, and claw trophies, when Leonard Johnson, the self-appointed master of ceremonies, noticed Ernie sitting all alone by the fire half-dozing, taking no notice of their fun.

Leonard felt gregarious. And brave. He stepped over to Ernie and spoke with great good cheer. "Ern, old boy, you never join in our storytelling. These guys are boring me to death. Why don't you share one of your memorable hunts with us?"

Ernie declined quietly, assuring Leonard that he hadn't been hunting in a long time. Had nothing to tell.

"Oh, come come, Ern. Surely you can think back and favor us with a tale. Just one? Please, sir?"

"Hear, hear!" The others joined in behind Leonard. There was even a short burst of muffled applause, their way of applying subtle pressure on Ernie, a tactic not lost on the old hunter, of course, and then there was silence while Ernie fidgeted in his seat, coughed, folded and unfolded his *Wall Street Journal*. He was boxed in. He could tell them to go to hell. He was capable of that. But he didn't.

He looked around at them, scrunching his brow into deep furrows, thinking back, back, back. The silence increased. They all leaned toward him in great anticipation until finally he breathed a deep breath, and let it out. They were ready to hang on his every word. He relished the respectful silence and it appeared he was milking it for all it was worth, but he was not in the habit of telling stories, he was trying to get it straight in his mind. At last he began.

"It was in deepest, darkest Africa . . ." he began, narrowing his eyes at each member of the group in turn as he proceeded, which heightened their anticipation and intensified their collective attention. "Summer of 'fifty-seven. Damn hot one, too. But I could take the heat then. It'd kill me now, of course . . ."

His voice trailed off. He shook his head and lowered it, closing his eyes, as if not being the man he used to be embarrassed him, rendered him incapable of going on with the story. Either that or he was going to sleep.

"Yes, yes, go on, Ern." Leonard encouraged him. He raised his head and half-opened his eyes. A new spark flickered in them as he proceeded.

"We were stalking the king of beasts—the lord of the jungle. The lion."

He had them now. My goodness, the suspense in the room was so tangible you could cut it with a knife. Not one of them had ever killed a lion. Old Ern was growing in stature right before their eyes. They loved it. They licked their lips, it was so good, and they were so boozy in their buckskin brotherhood.

"We were in the thickest part of the jungle," Ernie went on, "and sweat ran down my face. Not just because it was so awful, dreadful hot, but I was scared, I tell you. Scared to death. You couldn't see two feet in front of you. The native drums beat. My heart beat. We swung our machetes back and forth, hacking and parting, hacking and parting—forging our way through reeds and vines and tall elephant grass—getting closer, ever closer, to our prey."

The Hunt Club boys were totally entranced now, afraid to breathe for fear of losing a word. The spark in Ernie's eyes roared into flame, making his face glisten, alive with old energy. He raised his hand and pointed dramatically into the space before him. Seeing it.

"Suddenly, there he was—right in front of my face, so close I could have touched him! That massive head, hair matted. Yellowed teeth and foul, stinking breath. Eyes wild. He opened his mouth and roared a loud RRROAREEOWW!"

Ernie screamed the gutteral "Roar!" so loud he raised out of his chair, making the men jump back. Then his eyes swept heavenward, dolefully and painfully, and he muttered, "Oh, my," and slumped back in his chair.

Leonard couldn't stand it. "What did you do then, Ern?" he said.

"I—I'm—I'm ashamed to say," Ernie said. "I'm afraid I filled my pants."

He covered his mouth with his hand, embarrassed.

Leonard was quick with sympathy. He said, "Hey, Ern, it's nothing to be ashamed of. Why, I'm sure any one of us would have done the same in your situation, facing a big lion like that, why—"

"No, no," Ernie broke in. "I mean I filled my pants just *now* when I went RRROAREEOWW!"

Kin Vassy
NASHVILLE, TENNESSEE
and Billy Edd Wheeler

The Quick and the Dead

These two fellows down in North Carolina went bear hunting. They had heavy boots, hunting coats, high-powered rifles and all. They tramped around most of the day, went way back in the mountains. Finally they saw a big bear and both of them took aim. One of them nicked him and made him mad. He started for them at a lope, growling. This one guy threw down his rifle, pulled some track shoes out of his pack and started putting them on. The other one said, "Don't be silly. You can't outrun a bear."

"I don't have to. I just have to outrun you."

Loyal Jones

That'll Show Him

A group of hunters from the city went into the country to deer-hunt. One of them knew a farmer and said he would ask him if they could hunt on his land. They drove up to the farmhouse, and the leader went in to talk to the farmer. They talked for a while, and the farmer said he'd be glad to have them hunt on his land, but then he asked a favor. "I have this old mule out there in the pasture, and he's in bad shape, needs to be put out of his misery, but I've had him all his life and I just can't bear to shoot him. I wonder if you boys would shoot him for me. I'll bury him while you're hunting." The hunter thought he'd have some fun with his friends, and so when he got back to their car, he took out his deer rifle and said, "That miserly S.O.B. won't let us hunt on his land, and I'm going to get even with him. I'm going to shoot his mule."

He took off into the pasture, took aim, and shot the mule. Then he heard two more shots. He looked around and saw one of his friends standing there with a smoking gun. "We showed him," the man said. "I just shot two of his cows for good measure."

Loyal Jones

International Distress Signal

There was this old boy who had always wanted to go hunting but he was always afraid of getting lost. Nothing he did ever went right, you see, and he came by that genetically, because his daddy had been a genuine Kentucky-born loser. That's right, his daddy had M&Ms melt in his hand, he got run over with a Welcome Wagon, and when he died he had himself cremated. And on the way to his final resting place, the hearse got stuck in a snowdrift and they had to use his daddy's ashes to get unstuck!

Well, a friend of this old boy's said to him, "Now listen, you don't have to worry about getting lost during the hunting season. The woods are full of hunters, and if you ever get lost all you have to do is just get out in a clearing and shoot in the air three times. That's the international distress signal, and them hunters will quit what they're doing and come seek you out. If you're there longer than a half-hour, shoot in the air three more times! There's no way in the world you can stay lost in the hunting season more than an hour!"

It restored his confidence and he went out and bought the whole works. He got them L.L. Bean boots, he got them waterproof pants, and he got that coat, you know, and that Chippewa checkered shirt, and that duck-billed cap with the earmuffs on it—he got it all together! And he's so happy!

Soon he was out there hunting—I mean he was in the woods five minutes—and all of a sudden he's *lost*. So he got himself into a clearing and shot into the air three times and waited another half-hour and no one came. Then he shot into the air three more times, and *then* he knowed he was in a *world* of trouble, because he was down to his last two *arrows!*

Dr. Tim Stivers
LOUISVILLE, KENTUCKY

"*I Ain't Lost*":

MOUNTAINEERS AND CITY FOLKS

No Fool

This city fellow was driving down through the mountains when he got lost. He saw a farmer standing near the road behind his pasture fence. He stopped his car and asked, "How far to Knoxville?"

"Don't know."

"Well, how far is it to Lexington?"

"Don't know."

"You don't know much, do you?"

"Well, *I* ain't lost."

This angered the city man, and he said, "There isn't much between you and a fool, is there?"

"No, sir, just a fence," the farmer said.

Jim Ralston
PAINT LICK, KENTUCKY and PARADISE VALLEY, ARIZONA

Just Like Me

It seems there was this man who traveled the mountains, and back then you could stop at somebody's house and they would share with you. Well, this fellow was traveling along, and he was about to die of thirst, since it was hot and dry. He was mortally about to perish. He saw this old woman out hoeing corn, so he stopped and asked, "Ma'am, can I dip from your well?"

"Why certainly, son," she said. "Over there is the gourd dipper. Just help yourself."

Well, he stepped back a little bit and let her get back to hoeing corn before he picked up the dipper, because he had noticed that she had been dipping snuff, and it had run down her chin. It was disgusting. He stood and looked, trying to see if she was left-handed or right-handed, so he'd know which side of the dipper to drink from. He couldn't hardly tell, but finally he looked down at the gourd and noticed that there was a hole in the end of the handle. So he dipped it full of water, turned it up, and was drinking out of the handle when that old woman came around the corner of the house and exclaimed, "Well, Lord have mercy, Mister. You're the first person I ever seen that drinks water out of a gourd dipper just like I do!"

Mary Peterson
COSBY, TENNESSEE

No Two Ways About It

There is a guy called Kenneth Anderson, a mechanic, around Hayesville and Brasstown, North Carolina. You've seen these guys who are born geniuses, people that haven't been too far in school but are bright, sharp as a tack? Kenneth Anderson is one of them. He knows more about electricity and refrigeration and all kinds of engines than anybody around there. People who break down in that part of the world—big tractor-trailers—when they go to a garage to get it repaired, they'll refer them to Kenneth Anderson. Well, we were standing around his place one day, just standing there about closing time. We were dirty, covered with grease, smoking cigarettes, and this great big old car came rolling up and stopped. This guy rolled down his electric window, puffing on a big cigar, and said, "Do any of you know anything about air conditioning?" All of us—just like monkeys on a limb—turned and looked at Kenneth. Kenneth threw down his cigarette and said, "Well, I know one thing. It shore is good!" So that man rolled up his window and drove away.

Fred Park
BEREA, KENTUCKY

Funny You Should Ask

This old man was sitting by the side of the road and a lost tourist drives up and asks rather rudely, "How do you get to Boone?"

The old man takes his pipe out of his mouth and says, "Well, sometimes I walk, and sometimes my son-in-law takes me in his pickup truck."

William E. Lightfoot
BOONE, NORTH CAROLINA

Helping the Sightseers

When I was ten or eleven years old, I was sitting out on our porch picking on my banjo. Here come a great big station wagon with Eastern plates on it, car full of people. They pulled up in the yard, drove over my mother's flowerbed, and all got out and walked up to me. The daddy had his camera strapped on him, and he said, "You mind if we take your picture?"

I said, "No, I don't mind."

He asked, "Would you take your shoes off?"

I said, with a big smile, "I will if you will."

Well, he just sort of laughed at that. Then he said, "Our guidebook says here that Cherokee County has a rather remarkable blue marble courthouse. Have you ever heard of that?"

I mused over that a little, mumbling, "Courthouse, courthouse," and after a while I said, "Well, let me see, yes, I think I know where that is."

He said, "Could you tell us how to get there?"

I said, "Yeah, you go right down to that traffic light you can see down there. Go on past that light and go to the second one and take a left. You won't have any trouble."

He thanked me and they all got back in their car and drove down the street. Well, six years passed, or seven, or eight, and I finally got my driver's license, and the first thing I did was set out down that road to find out where the second traffic light was. It was in Cleveland, Tennessee—ninety-eight miles away!

Jan Davidson
CULLOWHEE, NORTH CAROLINA

Incompatibility

A woman tourist from up North asked a Tennessee lady for her cornbread recipe. She refused to give it. "With your accent, honey, it wouldn't be fit to eat anyway."

Charles Kirby
OAK RIDGE, TENNESSEE

Unscrupulous

The tourists are so gullible down our way that two old boys I know started bleaching coffee grounds and selling them for grits.

Max Woody
OLD FORT, NORTH CAROLINA

Easier That Way

A tourist drove in to a little Tennessee town and stopped at a service station for gas. He got out of his car while it was being serviced and looked the town over. "Any big people born here?" he asked.

"Naw," said the station attendant. "Just babies."

Loyal Jones

Monkey Business

Mrs. Daisy Morgan of Dayton, Tennessee, who survived well into her eighties, lived most of her life across the street from the Rhea County courthouse, site of the infamous evolution trial of 1925. The trial was held in Dayton after some local wags, who wanted to "put Dayton on the map," persuaded John Scopes, an earnest young teacher, to be a guinea pig for a staged and well-publicized "incident." Dubbed "Monkeytown" by H.L. Mencken, Dayton was often held up to ridicule for years after the affair. At a commemorative program in 1975, fifty years after the trial, Mrs. Morgan related this anecdote:

Tourists on their way to Florida often detoured off US 27 to circle the historic courthouse. "Have you got any monkeys around here?" the Yankee tourists sometimes yelled from their cars to the locals sitting in their front yards in the cool of the evening. "No," Mrs. Morgan said was the usual reply, "but we have a few who come off the highway and drive around the courthouse."

Bill Robinson
RICHMOND, KENTUCKY

Not Obvious

A country fellow went to the city and decided to go to a fancy restaurant. The prices were high and the portions skimpy. When he had finished, the waiter came and asked, "How did you find your steak?"

"Oh," he said, "I just turned over the potato, and there it was."

Oscar Davidson
SOMERSET, KENTUCKY

On Tippy Toes

Chet Atkins, Nashville's legendary guitarist, told me about taking his brother-in-law, Jethro Burns, to a ballet while they had some time to kill in Atlanta. Jethro had never seen a ballet, but was pretty impressed.

"Well, how did you like it?" Chet asked Jethro.

"Fine," he said. "I loved the costumes and the dancing, and all, but how come everybody was walking around on tippy-toes? Why don't they just get taller people?"

Billy Edd Wheeler

When in Rome

This Kentuckian went out to California to visit one of his relatives who had moved there. He liked it so well out there that he stayed for several months. One day he was talking with someone downtown, and to make conversation he asked, "How far is it to San José?" pronouncing the *J*.

"Out here," the fellow he was talking to said, "we say San Hos-ay. That's the way to pronounce Spanish words. How long have you been out here?"

"Oh, only since Hune or Huly," he said.

Virgil Catron
BEREA, KENTUCKY

Granny Goes to the City

The bellhop at the hotel was trying to help Granny but she was giving him a hard time. "Now, looky, young man, you may think I don't travel much because I'm from the hills. Well, the truth is, I don't, but still I ain't a plumb fool, and this-here room just won't do. There ain't no windows, it's too small and there's no bed. I want to talk to the manager right this minute."

"But, ma'am," the bellhop said. "This isn't your room, it's the elevator."

Granny went out for a walk but it was awfully hot on the city streets. Soon she came to a crowd of people gathered around a man who had fainted in the heat, and everybody was yelling out instructions. "Loosen his tie!" "Give him air!" "Give him a drink of water!"

Granny elbowed through and said, "Give him a drink of whiskey."

The suggestions kept coming hot and heavy and every so often Granny would shout, "Give him a drink of whiskey." The man finally raised up on his elbow and said, "Please, will all of you just shut up and listen to the little old lady!"

Granny walked into an automat and started dropping coins into the various food dispensers. Soon she had a table covered with sandwiches, pies and cakes, salads, puddings, fruit and an assortment of drinks. She searched her purse for the last of her change and dropped it into the coin-operated dispensers, cackling with laughter. The manager, who had been observing her all the while, finally walked over and asked her for an explanation. She didn't like his tone of voice.

"What's the matter," Granny said, "are you upset with me because I'm winning?"

After having a good lunch in the park and feeding the rest of the food to the squirrels and pigeons, Granny started walking back to the hotel. Suddenly a hold-up man jumped from behind some bushes and demanded her money.

"I ain't got no money left," she said, but he didn't believe her and proceeded to search her thoroughly. After searching her from top to bottom he grumbled, "I guess you were telling the truth. I can't find a penny on you."

"Well, don't stop searching, for goodness' sakes," Granny said. "I could write you a check."

Fresh from being searched and feeling a little light-headed, Granny crossed a busy street against traffic but somehow managed to make it safely to the other side. A policeman saw it all, came glaring up to Granny, spoke gruffly, "Didn't you see that sign?"

"What sign?" Granny asked.

"That DON'T WALK sign. It was flashing big as everything on that traffic signal."

"Oh yes, Officer," Granny said. "I saw it all right. But I thought it was an advertisement for a bus company."

Billy Edd Wheeler

Miracle Machine

A backwoods fellow and his son went to Lexington on business and found themselves in a tall building with an elevator. They watched as a hefty woman, beyond middle age, entered the conveyance and the doors closed. They observed the flashing lights that went from 1 to 10 and then back again, reacted with astonishment as the doors opened and a slender and beautiful young woman emerged. The old man grabbed his son by the arm and said, "Come on, boy, let's go get your ma and run her through that thing."

Paul Nester
LEXINGTON, KENTUCKY

Pretty Awesome

These two boys wanted to see the ocean and they hitchhiked until they were standing right on the sand, looking out over the sea for the first time. They were just awestruck. Finally one of them spoke: "Man, look at all that water!"

The other boy said, "And that's just the *top* of it!"

Dr. Carl Hurley
LEXINGTON, KENTUCKY

Fastest Squirrel Alive

A mountaineer went to town for the first time in forty years to look for a new plowpoint. In a hardware store he saw a big electric fan running and stood looking at it for a long time, amazed.

When the clerk came over to him he said, "That shore is a mighty fast squirrel you got in that cage!"

Billy Edd Wheeler

It May Be a Coffee-Grinder to You

I went to see a man named Mr. Dewey who was going to teach me how to tie trout flies. He showed me all the stuff he worked with—some fur, feathers, string, and all the little hooks he used to tie them on. After a couple of hours he said, "Now, son, I want to show you right here what is the biggest boon to fly-tying that the world has ever produced." He went out of the room and came back carrying one of these little German-made high-tech, cylindrical coffee-grinders that stand about that high, got a bubble top and a button; you put your coffee in there and it goes *zzzzzzip* and it's powder. He sat that thing down there and said, "I bet you don't know what that is! That's a fur blender. You know, if you want your imitation fly to look like a real one, you gotta get the color just right. Sometimes you can't just use the pure fur; you gotta blend fur. So you take the top off of that thing, put in a pinch of your gray squirrel fur, a pinch of red fox, a pinch of this and a pinch of that, and just mash that button, *zzzzzzip,* and run that around there until you got the right color and get them all blended up and just what you need."

I said, "That's amazing!"

He said, "You ever seen anything like it?"

I said, "Mr. Dewey, you aren't going to believe this, but I got one."

"You blend fur?"

I said, "Mr. Dewey, I grind coffee in mine."

He yelled into the kitchen, "Mama, he's got one of these! Guess what he does with it? He grinds coffee with it!"

She yelled back, "With what?"

He said, "His fur blender!"

She said, "Well, I'll be!"

Jan Davidson
CULLOWHEE, NORTH CAROLINA

"Could've Been This, Doc—":

HEALTH AND MEDICINE

No Shortage of Babies

A man and a woman showed up once a year at the hospital to have a baby. After about the eighth or ninth one, the doctor gave them a talk on contraceptives and gave them a supply, but the next year they showed up again with the wife ready to deliver. The doctor delivered the baby and then sat down with them for a talk. "Did you use the contraceptives I gave you?"

"Yes."

"Well, what do you think happened?"

"Could've been this, Doc. We don't have an organ, so we put those things on the piano."

Lucy Dail
MADISONVILLE, TENNESSEE

Shouldn't Limit Himself

A woman went regularly to the Red Bird Mission Hospital in Kentucky to have a baby. After the eighth one the doctor told her and her husband that they should not have any more babies, since she was in poor health. A year later, however, they turned up again, the wife ready to deliver. The doctor went ahead and delivered the ninth baby and then sat down with the husband for a stern talk. "Why did you not take my advice and quit having babies?"

"Well, Doc, I figure that a feller ought to use the talents God gave him."

Rev. Carl Eschbach
BEREA, KENTUCKY

More Babies

A doctor had been called to a rural house in north Georgia to deliver a baby. It was a poor family with many children, and he had never been paid for delivering any of them. After delivering the baby, he gave the father a lecture on abstinence and birth control. "You've got all of these kids, you don't have money to feed them, and, furthermore, you've never paid me for one of them." Came the next year, and the doctor was called to deliver another baby. He finished bringing it into the world and then cornered the father. "Why did you have another baby when you couldn't feed the ones you already had?"

"Doc," he said, "when the old woman gets me all stirred up, I feel like I could feed all the children in Georgia!"

Dr. Robert Johnstone
BEREA, KENTUCKY

Going Too Far

The patient was grateful to her psychiatrist and was greatly attached to him. One day she was overcome and said, "Kiss me, Doctor. Kiss me!"

"No, I can't do that," he said. "I shouldn't even be lying on the couch with you."

Rose Wheeler
BEREA, KENTUCKY

Quite an Idea

A farmer heard that an old friend had been deathly ill, and he went to see him. To his surprise when he got there his friend was sitting on the front porch looking well. "I hear you have been real sick," he said.

"Yes," the other replied, "but I'm better now."

"I hear that you can't eat a thing."

"Well, that was so, but I'm eating fine now. To tell the truth, I'm eating so much that I'm gaining weight. In fact, I've gained so much weight I can't see my penis."

"Is that so?" the man replied. "Then you ought to diet."

"What color?" the other one asked.

Wes Jackson
and Wendell Berry
PORT ROYAL, KENTUCKY

Medical History

A mountain woman came down to the university medical center for some tests. A doctor checked her over and then asked some questions. "Are you sexually active?" he asked.

"Well," she said, "I try to be as still as I can."

Karen Sexton
LEXINGTON, KENTUCKY

Keeps You Moving

The late Dr. Robert Cowley, college physician at Berea College, was visited by one of the maintenance workers. The man seemed in bad shape, and Dr. Cowley checked him over without finding anything obviously wrong with him. So he decided to ask some questions. "Do you drink coffee?"

"Yes, I do," the man said.

"How much?"

"Oh, I'd say about twenty cups a day."

"Twenty cups! Doesn't that keep you awake?"

"Well, it does help a little."

Dr. James S. Brown
LEXINGTON, KENTUCKY

Mighty Sick

A man had been away in the hospital, and when he came home, a friend inquired about his health. "Shucks," he said, "I's sick. Shucks, I's real sick. Shucks, I's so sick they put me in a room with bars on it to keep people from bothering me."

Jerry Plemmons
HOT SPRINGS, NORTH CAROLINA

Somebody's Got To Claim It

A man was taking tests in a hospital. A nurse asked him to bring a specimen to her in a bottle. He was shy, however, and he talked his wife into returning the bottle to the nurse.

"Is this urine?" the nurse asked.

"No, it's his'n."

Dan Greene
DAVID, KENTUCKY

Pay Attention

A man went to a doctor because of trouble with one of his eyes. "I got this piece of metal in my eye a long time ago, and it's begun to hurt me real bad," he explained.

"What year was that?" the doctor asked.

The man got upset and said, "It ain't my year, doctor. It's my eye."

Dr. Lee Morris
BEREA, KENTUCKY

Not Too Shrewd

A man had been sick, and he went to see a doctor. When he returned, his concerned neighbor came over and asked, "Did the doctor find out what you had?"

"No," he replied. "I had forty dollars in my pocket, and he only charged me ten."

Oscar Davidson
SOMERSET, KENTUCKY

Aqua Doc

I got sick and went to see a doctor. In a little while the nurse came out and said, "Doctor Papaboolaboolah will see you now."

I said, "Which doctor?"

She said, "Oh, no, he's fully qualified."

Anyway, I ended up having a kidney transplant. About a week later I found out the donor was a bed-wetter.

James Clifford Terry
KNOXVILLE, TENNESSEE

Healthy Rural Life

We live here for our health, here at Wildcat Rock City. It's the healthiest place you've ever seen. It's so far to the doctor, that if you're going to get well at all, you'll get well before you get there. We've started three or four times to the doctor, and we'd get well before we got there, and turn around and come back.

We went one day to the doctor over in Whitley County, and the doctor was gone—good doctor he was too. We were ailing pretty bad. I said, this is it. We just knew we were going to die. We stopped out there a ways and got us something to eat, and I began to see Mabel's eyes pick up, and she said, "You look better." And I said I felt better. We came on down the road and stopped at a little store and got us something else to eat, and by doggies, she was a-pattin' her feet to dance before we got home. But as we were coming on back, we met my brother-in-law. He'd been ailing too. He was feeling mighty weak, looking awful bad. I told him what to do. I said, "You go and get you something to eat, and you'll get to feeling better." It was malnutrition, and we didn't know it! We'd starved and thought it was some kind of disease we'd caught. We found out it was nothing but starvation. Now, most of the time when we get to feeling bad, we get us something to eat, and we get all right. Most of the people around here are so stingy, they won't eat what they want.

Virgil Anderson
ROCKY BRANCH, KENTUCKY

"We May Be Crazy but We're Not Stupid":

RURAL LIFE

A Brilliant Idea

This man had a flat tire next to the insane asylum. He jacked up his wheel, took it off, put the nuts in his hubcap, and put it up on his hood. They fell off into his grill, and he couldn't get them out. He thought, "Oh, Lordy. What am I going to do?"

Across the fence one of the inmates was watching him and said, "Just take one nut off of each of the other wheels and put them on that one, and it'll get you where you're going."

He said, "That's a brilliant idea. Why, you're not crazy. What are you doing in there?"

"I may be crazy, but I'm not stupid."

Billy Wilson
BEREA, KENTUCKY

Waste Not, Want Not

My grandfather used to say that he got more out of his tobacco than anybody else. He would chew it, dry it, and smoke it, snuff the ashes up his nose, then blow his nose and polish his shoes.

Max Woody
OLD FORT, NORTH CAROLINA

Fast-Growing Vines

The other day this lady called a radio talk show, and from the way she talked, the disc jockey thought she must be a newcomer to the area. She said, "I wonder if any of the folks listening out there today could direct me to where I could get a few cuttings of kudzu?"

The disc jockey said, "Ma'am, you're within the sound of my voice, let me clarify this, and you don't have any kudzu in your yard?"

She said, "That's right."

He said, "Well, just wait a few minutes."

Jan Davidson
CULLOWHEE, NORTH CAROLINA

It Was Complex

Back during World War II, two old-timers who lived far back in the mountains fell to talking. One asked the other, "How is the war going in Europe?"

"Well, I don't know too much about it, but I hear that the English are beating the hell out of the British."

Wilma Dykeman
NEWPORT, TENNESSEE

A Driving Curiosity

Once there was this fellow who was a little "teched." He'd never been out of his little town. As a matter of fact he had never even had a ride in a truck, but he admired the big trucks that went in and out of town.

One day he asked a guy if he could take a ride with him, and he said, "Yes, be here at ten o'clock tomorrow morning and I'll take you for a ride." The fellow that drove the truck left at nine. The next day the fellow said, "I thought you were going to take me for a ride." The driver said, "Well, okay, be here tomorrow morning at nine." Then he left at eight.

Well, the guy got a jump on him and got there at four o'clock the third day and caught him. He said, "I want to go riding with you!" The driver said, "Okay, get in the truck." They rode for a while and then they came to a small town that had one red light—they didn't really need it, just put one up anyway. Just as the driver came up to it, it changed to red, and he slammed on his brakes and that little "teched" fellow was jolted up somewhat and asked, "What's going on?"

The driver said, "Well, I had to stop for that red light!"

The fellow rolled his window down, reached his head out, and looked up and around and yelled, "Oh, you can bring it on through. You'll clear it by three or four feet!"

Bruce Fraley
BEREA, KENTUCKY

Nosy

There were a lot of people in this restaurant and one of them had one of the biggest, highest noses you ever saw. It was an awful big, long nose. He was a big bony-faced fellow, I guess six-and-a-half feet tall—a big man. Well, the waitress came around and saw him and couldn't help asking how come his nose was so big.

He said, "Madam, I kept it out of other people's business until it got its growth."

Henry Matney
and William E. Lightfoot
BOONE, NORTH CAROLINA

Homemade Money

Making good moonshine is hard work, so when this moonshiner heard his city cousin talking about how easy it was to make counterfeit money, he decided to give it a go.

He printed up some bills, thought they looked pretty good, and decided to put them to the test. He went down to the country store, ordered a dollar's worth of chewing tobacco, and slapped a brand new nineteen-dollar bill on the counter.

The storekeeper glanced at it, said to him, "How do you want your change, buddy, three sixes or two nines?"

Billy Edd Wheeler

Good Quality

We've had this axe in the family for two hundred years, and it's only had four new handles and two new heads.

George Wolford
ASHLAND, KENTUCKY

The High-Tech Girdle

One summer day I was getting ready to go to West Union—that's where I'm from—and I was having trouble getting my girdle on. So I called for my son to bring the fan, the only one that wasn't a rolled-up newspaper. I was going to stand in front of that fan, you know, and turn around so it could keep me dried off so I could pull my girdle up.

My son brought the fan up and set it down asking, "What do you want with this?"

I said, "Well, so I can get my clothes on."

He said, "Oh, no, don't tell me you have to blow that thing up to get it on!"

Bonnie Collins
WEST UNION, WEST VIRGINIA

Long Gone

Two women met and one inquired about another whom she hadn't seen in a long time. "Oh, haven't you heard? She's gone to the Holy Land."

"My goodness," the first woman exclaimed. "How long was she sick?"

Dr. Mary Pauline Fox
PIKEVILLE, KENTUCKY

Just Enough

What people said about Aunt Becky was that she was almost stingy. She carried that Scotch-Irish thriftiness to a near fault. It was hard for the neighbors to understand because she had never lacked for much in her life. Her husband, Judge Felton, took sick and was about to die. This was back in the days before air conditioning, and she called Little Earl and said, "Earl, I want you to go down to the store and get some ice, because the Judge has got a high fever, and we need to put some ice around him to keep him cool. Here is a nickel."

Earl said, "Aunt Becky, a nickel's worth of ice won't last the night."

She looked at Earl and said, "Neither will the Judge."

Charlotte Ross
BOONE, NORTH CAROLINA

Job Benefits

Soon after I became president of Berea College, a friend of mine asked, "How's your new job?"

I said, "Oh, it's great. I work hard all day, but I go home and sleep like a baby—sleep two hours, wake up and cry, sleep two hours, wake up and cry."

Dr. John Stephenson
BEREA, KENTUCKY

Regretful

A man's father died, leaving no will and many complications with the estate. The son hired a good lawyer and after many months got everything worked out. "Well," said the lawyer to his client. "This has been an ordeal for you, hasn't it?"

"Yeah," he replied, "sometimes I wish the old man hadn't died."

Loyal Jones

Pretty Sharp

Caleb Smith, a Missionary Baptist preacher, and Abel Smith (no relation), a Primitive Baptist elder, of Tennessee, were old friends. One day when they were visiting with one another in town, Abel said to Caleb, "Caleb, do you see that fly walking across the little hand of the clock across yonder on the courthouse?"

Caleb looked for a time at the clock, a good hundred yards away, cupped his hand to his ear, and said, "No, Abel, I can't see it, but I know it's there for I can hear it a-walking."

Dr. Louis Smith
BEREA, KENTUCKY

One Lesson Is Enough

You don't learn anything from the second kick of a mule.

Governor Bert T. Combs
LEXINGTON, KENTUCKY

Logistics Problem

This man from back in the country went down to the county road department and applied for a job. They put him to painting those yellow lines down the middle of the highway. The first day he did a good job, painted about two miles. The second day he painted only about a mile, and the third day he did only about a half a mile. So the boss said they'd have to let him go. They paid him off, but before he left he said, "You know it ain't my fault. It was just too far back to the paint can."

Loyal Jones

Sort of Lazy

He was fascinated with work. He could sit and watch it for hours.

Dr. Joseph Taylor
INDIANAPOLIS, INDIANA

Amateurs

This fellow got interested in sky-diving, and he went to the local county-seat airport and asked if he could try it. A pilot said he would take him up and showed him what to do to get his parachute to open. He said it was simple, that all he had to do was to pull the ring. They took off and flew up to about ten thousand feet, and the pilot opened the door and told him to jump. He was scared, but he jumped. He fell a few hundred feet, and then he pulled the ring. Nothing happened. He fell on down, tugging his ring. Then he saw a man flying up from the ground, his arms and legs all waving. When the man got close to him, he yelled, "Know anything about parachutes?"

"No," the man yelled back. "Know anything about boilers?"

Chris Kermiet
DENVER, COLORADO

Getting Above His Raising

A mountaineer got rich running a coal mine. He and his wife moved to Lexington to live. They worked on their accents, their haircuts and clothes, wanting to fit in and not let anybody know that they were country folks. One evening they decided to go to a restaurant. He ordered an entree, and then in his newly acquired accent said, "Bring us, tomahtoes, potahtoes, and beans." They ate, and when the bill came, it was enormous, this being a classy restaurant. He looked in disbelief at the bill and said, "This is the first time I ever paid forty dollars for 'maters, taters, and beans!"

Diana Hays
BEREA, KENTUCKY

Not Afraid to Work

Times got so bad during the Depression that my cousin went down to the post office and applied for the job on the poster that said "Man Wanted For Robbery."

Loyal Jones

That's Poor

I'm from a big family—and I hate to tell you how poor we were—but one time when my brother swallowed a dime, I followed him around for three days with a stick!

Roni Stoneman
NASHVILLE, TENNESSEE

Heavy Lunch

Back in the Depression this little boy didn't have anything to take to school for lunch except turnips. His mother boiled them, fried them, and baked them, but he got so tired of turnips that he didn't think he could eat another one. One day during a recess before lunch the boy decided to steal somebody else's lunch while everybody was on the playground for a ball game. He sneaked out of the game and went into the schoolhouse where the students kept their lunches on a shelf. He weighed all of the bags in his hand and ran out behind the school with the heaviest one. He was excited as he opened it, and what do you think he found? Three hickory nuts and a clawhammer!

Vic Naylor
LEXINGTON, KENTUCKY

That's Poor

We were so poor when I was a kid that I didn't have any clothes, but when I was fourteen, they bought me a hat and let me look out the window.

Louis Marshall ''Grandpa'' Jones
MOUNTAIN VIEW, ARKANSAS

Benefits of Fire and Flood

The late Willie Dawahare, oldest of the famous eastern Kentucky department store family, told of going to Las Vegas one spring after one of the great floods had devastated eastern Kentucky, including his Hazard store. He planned to take a vacation while his store was being cleaned up and restocked. One night he met a nice man from New York, and they fell to talking. ''What business are you in, Sam?'' asked Willie.

''I run a department store,'' said Sam.

''But it is nearly Easter, one of the busiest times of the year. Why are you in Las Vegas now?''

''Well, I had a fire,'' he said. ''And by the way, Willie, what do you do?''

"I run a department store too."

"Well, what are you doing out here this close to Easter?"

"I had a flood," Willie said.

Sam then said, "Willie, how do you start a flood?"

Willie Dawahare
HAZARD, KENTUCKY

Nice Not To Have To Be Careful

Even in the most adverse situations, someone in Kentucky will have something funny to say, like this old boy down in Eddyville State Penetentiary where he was on Death Row. He was going to be executed the next day. Well, they came in there that evening and said it was time for his last meal, said he could have anything he wanted. "Well," he said, "I reckon I'd like a mess of them there mushrooms."

They said, "That's good. They'll taste good on a nice steak. You want one of them too, don't you?"

He said, "No, I just want mushrooms."

"Why in the world would you want just mushrooms?" they asked.

"Well, to tell you the truth," he said, "up to now, I've always been afraid to try them."

Dr. Tim Stivers
LOUISVILLE, KENTUCKY

Home in Indiana

"What is a Hoosier?"

"A Kentucky hillbilly who has car trouble on the way to Michigan."

Doug Crawford
BUSY, KENTUCKY

Right Is Wrong

A father and his son went fishing. When they got back and while the father was putting away his gear, the mother asked the boy how it had gone. ''Just terrible,'' he said. ''I did everything wrong. I talked too much, I used the wrong lures, I cast into the wrong places, and I caught twice as many fish as Dad.''

Loyal Jones

The Experts Are Unavailable

Exasperated man to his wife: ''It's a crying shame that the only people who know how to run this country are tending bar, cutting hair, or driving taxicabs.''

Loyal Jones

Something To See

''What has 23 teeth and 110 legs?''

''I don't know. What?''

''The front row at a Merle Haggard concert.''

Carol Elizabeth Reynolds
RABUN GAP, GEORGIA

Thanks All the Same

When I was a barber, a friend came in one day, said his father was in the hospital, and asked if I would go by after work and shave him. I said I'd be glad to. So I took my straight razor and some soap and went to the hospital. The old man was pretty sick and had quite a growth of beard. They didn't have any hot water, and I couldn't get his beard softened up too well. I went ahead and shaved him, scraped off his beard the best I could, thinking I was doing him a favor. When I finished, I said, ''If you're going to be in here a while and need another shave, I'll be glad to come and give you one.''

He looked up and said, ''Well, I don't guess I'll be calling you. I'll just set fire to it and burn it off. It won't hurt no worse.''

John Gilliam
BEREA, KENTUCKY

That Kind of a Guy

He's a good old boy, but . . .
—he's about two bricks shy of a load.
—he's a few pickles short of a jar.
—his elevator don't go all the way to the top.
—he's not wrapped too tight.
—his cheese has slid off his cracker.
—I don't believe his yeast rose.
—his lights are on but nobody's home.
—I believe he's got a short in his cord.
—he's about a bubble off of plumb.
—he's lost some of his marbles.
—all his marbles aren't rolling in the same groove.
—he's two dishes short of a picnic.

Carol Elizabeth Reynolds
RABUN GAP, GEORGIA

Good News and Bad

This man borrowed a friend's car, and when he came back, he said, "I've got some good news and some bad news."

"What's the bad news?"

"I ran your car over a cliff."

"What's the good news?"

"It got a hundred miles to the gallon going down."

Billy Wilson
BEREA, KENTUCKY

Neo-Texans

Two men in Texas were giving reasons for moving from Kentucky. "I moved because of my beliefs," said the first one.

"How's that?" asked the second.

"I believed the horse was mine."

Loyal Jones

Sympathy

A Kentucky mountain farmer was showing his farm to a wealthy cousin who had gone off to Texas and prospered and was now back for a visit. Whatever the Kentuckian showed him, the Texan had one that was bigger and better. As they walked down through a narrow creek bottom, the Texan asked, "How many acres do you own?"

"Eighty acres," the Kentuckian replied.

"Why, on my place," said the Texan, "I can get up in the morning, climb in my pickup, and drive all day, and that night I still won't be to the other side of my property."

"I understand," said the Kentuckian, "I used to have a pickup like that."

Raymond F. McLain
BEREA, KENTUCKY

Hell or Texas

Cratis Williams, the late venerable Appalachian scholar, once said that if you messed around with a mountain man's womenfolks in the old days and got caught, you had two choices: hell or Texas.

Dr. Cratis D. Williams
BOONE, NORTH CAROLINA

Hard To Get It Done Right

This fellow ate in the same restaurant every day, and he always complained about how the food was prepared. He had all sorts of strange requests in regard to his food, and nothing ever pleased him. One morning he ordered two eggs, one sunny-side-up and the other scrambled. The long-suffering waitress gave the order to the cook, and eventually brought the man's breakfast. He stared at the eggs for a long time and said, "He's scrambled the wrong one."

Oscar Davidson
SOMERSET, KENTUCKY

Contrary

We had a man down in my state who did not agree with anybody about anything. He found that cabbage didn't agree with him, and thereafter he wouldn't eat anything but cabbage.

Sen. Sam J. Ervin, Jr.
MORGANTON, NORTH CAROLINA

Quiet Day

A man was walking along and saw a fellow with his ear against the ground. When he got close, the fellow said, "Come here and listen."

So he went over, put his ear to the ground, and listened for a long while. "I don't hear a thing," he said.

"I know," the fellow said, "it's been like that all day."

Loyal Jones

No Equipment

A country fellow was going down a seedy street in the city when a fellow came up and asked, "Would you like to buy some pornography?"

"No," he said. "I don't even have a pornograph."

Charles Tribble
CYNTHIANA, KENTUCKY

Destiny

I know I was cut out for something big, but my mother must have sewed me up wrong.

Virgil Anderson
ROCKY BRANCH, KENTUCKY

Scared of Flying

"I'm not gettin' in none of them wind machinters."

"Now, Joe, it's nothing to worry about."

"I'm not flyin' in one of them egg-beaters. As long as I've got one foot on the ground, I know the other'n ain't fer from it."

"Look, we've got a good pilot. There's nothing to worry about. When the Good Lord gets ready for you, it doesn't matter whether you are up there or down here, you're going to go."

"I know that. But what if you and me are up there and the Good Lord calls the pilot. What's me and you goin' to do?"

"Old Joe" Clark
BEREA, KENTUCKY

Road Question

Why did the chicken cross the road?

To prove to possums that it could be done.

Staley Clements
CHRISTIANSBURG, VIRGINIA

An Unlicensed Psychic

This midget was going around to psychic fairs in different towns, conducting séances and stuff, and billed himself as a medium "Specializing in psychic analizations of created thought, devoted to synchronization of spiritual self and physical self to a conscious level . . . Channeled energy healing . . . Psychic surgery."

He became a fairly popular medium and hung out his shingle in this one town where he was arrested and put in jail for practicing without a license. After a while he managed to escape, and the headline read:

Small Medium at Large.

Chet Atkins
NASHVILLE, TENNESSEE

All the Modern Conveniences

"Ma'am, have you got running water?"

"Of course we've got running water, if you run from the spring to the house!"

Hannah McConnell
ROGERSVILLE, TENNESSEE

Well-Known Buyers

Just before Christmas, a man was out shopping with his wife. The salesman showed them some nice furniture, and they especially liked a certain living room suite. The husband said, "We like it, but I don't think we can afford it."

The salesman said, ''You make one small down payment and don't make another payment for six months.''

The wife jumped up and said, ''Who told you about *us?*''

Dr. Carl Hurley
LEXINGTON, KENTUCKY

Like Son, Like Father

The mountain boy announced to his dad as he went through the gate, ''I'm going off to look for adventure, prosperity, beautiful women, and excitement, and I'm on my way right now, so don't try to stop me.''

''Who's trying to stop you?'' his father said. ''Shucks, I think I'll go with you!''

Billy Edd Wheeler

No Identity Crisis Here

A mountain girl stood at the bank teller's window as the teller looked at her check, then asked her, ''Can you identify yourself?''

She reached into her purse, pulled out a mirror, looked at it, said, ''Yep, it's me, all right.''

Billy Edd Wheeler

One More Game

Die-hard golfers, otherwise normal human beings, often go to any lengths to get in a round of golf. They'll cancel important business meetings, skip meals, rearrange weddings (their own), funerals, fishing trips, whatever it takes. And some of them are so bad they have to be masochists to keep playing the game, it gives them so much pain and embarrassment.

One such man decided to kill himself, after a miserable

and devastating game, slashed his wrists, stood there alone in front of the mirrors over a sink in the locker room, watching the color drain from his face.

A man entered the locker room and saw him from behind, not realizing what was going on, yelled to him, "Hey, Fred, how about playing a round with us tomorrow!"

He looked up, slapped his wrists together, answered, "What time?"

Billy Edd Wheeler

Advice from a Hillbilly Golfer

I was playing golf with my old friend Goose Andrews just outside of Beckley, West Virginia, on a course that he built himself with a rake and a bulldozer. After hitting a fairly good drive on the first par-four on the front nine, I asked Goose what club most golfers used to get on the green from where I lay. (He was a stronger golfer than I, so I knew not to ask him what he would hit from there.)

"Most golfers use a seven-iron from there," Goose said. So I took out a seven and struck the ball nicely, only to watch it plop into the lake guarding the front of the green. Goose looked amused, but I didn't think it was so funny.

"I thought you said most golfers use a seven-iron from here," I said.

"They do," Goose replied. "And most of them go in the lake, just about where you did."

Billy Edd Wheeler

An Unforgettable Golf Score

A man was playing golf with his wife once on a fairly new course out in the country. On one hole he sliced the ball badly and ended up in the rough behind a barn they hadn't gotten around to removing from the course yet. He took out his pitching wedge and started to hit the ball when his wife stopped him. "What are you doing?"

"I thought I'd take this wedge and hit the ball back into the fairway, maybe at least bogey the hole," he told her.

"Don't be silly," she said. "Look, the barn doors are wide

open. You've got a good lie. Take your three-wood, hit it straight through the barn, and maybe you'll get a par or a birdie."

He put his pitching wedge back in the bag and took out his three-wood, addressed the ball, and hit it in the sweet spot, a shot that took off like a rifle bullet through the opening in the barn. A beauty. Except halfway through the barn corridor the ball hit a wooden beam and came flying back, hitting his wife in the left temple and killing her.

A few weeks later he was playing golf again with a buddy when, on the same hole, he sliced the ball to exactly the same place in the rough. He took out his pitching wedge and was about to hit the ball when his buddy ran over and stopped him. "What are you doing?"

"I thought I'd chip the ball out into the fairway," he said, "and maybe at least bogey the hole."

"Don't be stupid," the buddy said. "Look, the barn doors are wide open—you could drive a Mack truck through there. Take your three-wood, hit through the barn, you might save par or even birdie the hole."

"Huh-uh." The man shook his head sadly. "The last time I tried that I ended up taking a nine on this hole!"

Billy Edd Wheeler

Say That Again?

My mother, Mary Isabelle Stewart, works in the IGA store of Central City, Kentucky. One day a lady customer walked up to her and asked where she could find the Tampax.

My mother thought the lady said thumbtacks, so she asked her, "Did you want the kind you drive in with a hammer or the kind you push in with your thumb?"

The lady looked at my mother sideways, shook her head, and left the store.

Billy Edd Wheeler

Big Crop

Two farmers were always kidding one another about the size of their crops or livestock. One of them had a particularly good watermelon crop, and he told his son to go over to the other's house and borrow his crosscut saw to cut one of his melons with. After a while the boy came back and said, "He said he would be glad to loan you his saw but that he is using it now to saw open one of his cantaloupes."

Loyal Jones

Done

In the last century, a man from Ireland decided to emigrate to America. An old lady heard he was leaving and came to ask him where he was aiming for in the United States. He said he was going to Washington County, Virginia. "Well, she said. "I've got a son over there, and he hasn't written me in two years. His name is James Donne, and he lives in a little white house in back of a store. I would be obliged if you would look him up and tell him to write to me."

When the young man got to Washington County, he began to look for a store and found one. "Do you have a little house out back?" he asked.

"Yes, we do," the storekeeper said. "Go on back if you want to."

He went in back of the store and found the outhouse. He knocked on the door and inquired, "Are you Donne?"

A voice from inside answered, "Yes, I am."

"Well, write your mother," he said and left.

Loyal Jones

Partial Success

Two men were out in the field hoeing corn when a man came over in a hang glider. The glider made a big shadow, and one of the men looked up, grabbed his shotgun, and yelled, "That's the biggest chicken hawk I ever saw." He let go with both barrels. The second man never looked up but asked, "Did you get him?"

"No, but I made him turn that man loose."

Billy Wilson
BEREA, KENTUCKY

Quick

The blacksmith was shaping red-hot horseshoes on his anvil and throwing them down on the ground to cool. A local boy wandered up, reached down, and picked up one of the half-cooled shoes. He quickly dropped it. The blacksmith asked slyly, "Was it hot?"

"No, it just don't take me long to look at a horseshoe."

Jack Marema
BEREA, KENTUCKY

Common Sense

A farmer went over to see his neighbor and found him down at the barn sawing on a log that went above the door to his mule's stable. "Why are you doing that?" he asked.

"Because my mule hits his head on it every time he goes in or out of the stable."

"Well, why don't you dig the floor out. It would be easier than sawing that log."

"It ain't his feet that it's hitting. It's his head," the farmer said, and went on sawing.

Willis Jones
MARBLE, NORTH CAROLINA

Hot and Cold

We lived in Chattsworth, Georgia, population two hundred, and when I was six years old, my daddy came home from the military hospital in Atlanta at the end of World War II. He brought my grandparents a present, a Thermos bottle, big and shiny with a stainless steel cap. In the mountains we share things, set it out for people to look at. People came to see Daddy, and there was that Thermos bottle sitting on the front porch. After a while this woman came, sat down in a rocking chair, and eyed that Thermos bottle, the wheels in her head turning. "Ain't that thing a wonder, now?" my mama said. "In the summertime, we can fill that up with cold lemonade, and we can take it off on a picnic and it will keep that lemonade as cold till noontime as when we left the house."

The woman nodded. Then Mama said, "Of the wintertime, I can put soup in there, and it'll stay hot till noontime."

The woman thought and said, "How does it know which way to do?"

Charlotte Ross
BOONE, NORTH CAROLINA

How Far Back?

We lived so far back in the sticks that . . .

—the sun set between our house and the road.

—we had to use hoot owls for chickens.

—we had to go toward town to hunt.

—we had to grease the wagon three times to get to town.

—when my mother put the first necktie on my brother, he stood there all day thinking he was tied up.

Loyal Jones

Checking It Out

My father, who lives in Lee County, Virginia, picked up a fellow one day who was known for living off the land, so to speak. As they rode along, they passed an abandoned house which had several stands of bees in the yard. The man asked my father whose bees they were. "They belonged to So-and-so," he said, "but he's dead now."

They rode along in silence for a while, the man thinking, and then he said, "Well, he wouldn't be needing them anymore, would he?"

Dr. Bill Friar
DAYTON, OHIO

Take Your Pick

There was a fellow who went down and got a job on the railroad. He took a jar of honey with him to eat. While he was gone, these fellows hid his honey. He came back and said, "Hey, you fellers, my honey's gone." They said they didn't know anything about it. He hunted around there a couple of hours, trying to find it. Finally he got mad. And he was mean. He came back and said, "Look here, boys. Some of you damn fellers has got my honey. Now I've fooled with you all morning, and I'm telling you right now you've got three choices—honey, money, or hell!"

Virgil Anderson
ROCKY BRANCH, KENTUCKY

A Right Fancy Dinner

This farmer and his wife belonged to a garden club that once a week took turns having dinner at somebody's house. When it got to be their turn they discussed the menu and decided on steak, gravy, and mushrooms. The farmer, being a practical man, said, "Shucks, we can save some money, too. We got mushrooms growing all over the place. Let's pick our own. They're just as good as store bought ones, maybe better."

"They might be poison, honey," his wife argued. "It's hard to tell the difference in edible mushrooms and poison toadstools."

"Well, then, let's hire us a cook from town. She'll know, and besides she'll give the party a touch of class."

The town cook arrived that morning, but she wasn't sure about the mushrooms. Then she got an idea: "Let's sauté a few of them in butter and feed them to your dog. I'll keep an eye on him for a few hours while we're preparing the appetizers and main course, and if they don't bother him we'll know they're okay."

The farmer called old Spot. The cook fed him the mushrooms. He slurped them up, went back to playing and chasing cats all afternoon, so they felt pretty safe about eating the mushrooms for dinner.

It was an elegant dinner, served up by the town cook, and folks bragged in particular about the mushrooms and gravy. Superb! But in the middle of dessert the cook came running in with horror in her face, announced: "Old Spot is dead!"

Pandemonium struck. People started sweating and rubbing their stomachs, pacing the floor nervously, sobbing and crying and praying out loud, and soon the doctor rushed out from town and screeched up the drive, throwing gravel all over the porch, and started taking pulses and pumping stomachs and handing out aspirins.

By the time he had attended to just about everybody and things had quieted down some, the town cook came back into the room and said, "I think it was terrible that that guy that ran over old Spot never even slowed down. Just kept on going."

Billy Edd Wheeler
and Chet Atkins
NASHVILLE, TENNESSEE

Just Write It Down

My stepfather, Arthur Stewart, called me once from a pay phone somewhere in Boone County, West Virginia, to give me the number of my brother, Bob Stewart. He said, "It's PU7-4026."

I couldn't hear him too plainly, so I asked him, "Was that P as in Peter?"

"What?" he replied.

I said, "Was that P as in Peter or Paul or Philip?"

"I don't know nothing about that," he said, "it's just PU7-4026."

Billy Edd Wheeler

Long-Term

A couple had saved their money for years so that they could build a new house. Finally they had enough, and they went to the building supplies store to start buying materials. They ordered two hundred two-by-fours. "How long do you want them?" the clerk asked. "Oh, we want them for a long time," the woman said, "we're building a house."

Loyal Jones

The Parachute That Didn't Open

A mountain boy joined the paratroopers and was listening intently to the instructor just before his first jump.

"When you jump, count to ten, then pull this ripcord. Your chute will open and you'll float gently down to earth. Now, if for some reason the chute doesn't open, don't worry.

Just pull this handle here; it's your emergency ripcord. Your chute will open and you'll float right down. Now, any questions?"

The mountain boy held up his hand. "Uh, sir, after we land we're gonna be thirty miles out in the boondocks. How are we gonna get back?"

"Don't worry," the instructor said, "there'll be a truck there to pick you up and bring you back to the base."

So they took off and the boy jumped, counted to ten, and pulled the cord. Nothing happened. So he pulled the emergency cord, and again nothing happened. As he was falling toward the earth he thought to himself, "Dang it, the way things are going, I'll bet that truck won't be there, neither!"

Dr. Arthur M. Bannerman
SWANNANOA, NORTH CAROLINA

The Choice

I had stopped at Miller's Store in Haw Creek one summer day to get an RC and there was a bunch of guys on the porch of the feed, seed, and hardware side listening to a young man bragging about his new car, a Hudson Hornet. This in the days before the Japanese invasion when the only car or truck anybody owned was a Ford or Chivlay.

The boy just went on and on about his new Hudson, how it would do 85 wide open, and so on, and finally one old man asked if it was true what he heard about the first night when the boy had brought his new car home.

"I heerd he was so proud of that Hudson," the old man turned to the other guys, "that the first night he chained the front bumper to the outhouse so nobody could steal his new car—and when he went out early the next morning, somebody had cut the chain and stole the outhouse!"

Joe Bly
ASHEVILLE, NORTH CAROLINA

All There by a Hair's Breadth

A farmer sold his tobacco at the warehouse in Asheville, North Carolina, and headed to the bank to cash his check. It was for six thousand eight hundred forty-eight dollars and twenty-two cents.

The teller gave him the cash and he stepped to one side to count it. Then he counted it again, shook his head, and counted it again. As he stood there thinking about counting it one more time the teller, who had noticed him counting and recounting, said, "Sir, isn't it all there?"

"Yes," the farmer replied. "But it jist is!"

Billy Edd Wheeler

Competent

A county agricultural extension agent and a rural sociologist from the university (actually Mike Duff and Ralph Ramsey) were sitting in the University of Kentucky Extension office in Elliott County, Kentucky, feet upon their desks, talking when a man came in looking for a job. They decided to do some vocational counseling on the spot. "What kind of work can you do?" one of them asked.

"I can do 'most anything."

"Do you know how to run a farm?"

"Yep."

"Can you do mechanics?"

"Yeah, I can do that."

"Can you do carpentry?"

"Yep."

"If you had a choice, what kind of work would you like to do?"

After looking over the office and staring at the two professionals, he said, "Well, if I had my druthers, I'd just as soon do what you fellers are doing as anything I can think of."

Dr. Mike Duff
LEXINGTON, KENTUCKY

Feline Consultant

This small town had a problem with cats. There were stray cats everywhere, hanging around everybody's back door, in the garbage and generally being a great nuisance. The mayor called a meeting of the town council to discuss the problem. "I think," said one member, "that we ought to write a grant and get us some consultants to come down here and study this problem." Everybody thought this was a good idea, so the mayor appointed a committee to write a proposal to one of the big foundations. The foundation not only gave them the money but recommended two consultants (who of course had once worked for the foundation). They contacted the consultants, who came down, set up shop, applied their vast knowledge to the situation, wrote a report, and asked for a meeting with the town council. The whole town turned out to hear the report. "You know that huge yellow tabby tomcat that struts up and down the main street?" one of the consultants asked. Everybody knew the cat. "Well, we've determined that he is the sire of two-thirds of the cats in town. Our recommendation is that you have that cat neutered, and your cat problem will be over."

The local veterinarian volunteered his services, the cat was caught and the operation performed. The cat population dwindled, and all was well for several years. Then the cats again began multiplying rapidly. The mayor called the council together again, and they decided once more to write a proposal in order to get the consultants back again. They were successful and the consultants once again set up shop. After a careful study, they were ready to present their findings, and again the whole town came. "You know that huge yellow tabby cat that struts up and down the main street?" the consultant asked. "Well, we've found that he is the problem."

The veterinarian jumped up and shouted, "I resent that. You are impugning my professional integrity. I fixed that cat so that it is impossible for him to cause any more kittens in his lifetime!"

"You don't understand," said the expert. "He's become a consultant!"

Loyal Jones

Esoteric-Exoteric Dimensions of Appalachian Folk Humor

WILLIAM E. LIGHTFOOT
Associate Professor of English
Appalachian State University

One of the first lessons I learned as a student of folklore was that jokes not only provide opportunities for laughter but carry substantial psychosocial weight as well. During the second week of his introductory graduate course at Indiana University called "Proseminar in Folklore Theory and Techniques," Richard Dorson asked students to collect and analyze a joke, without giving us any advice whatsoever, whether theoretical or technical, on how to go about doing it. As it happened, I stumbled onto the "technique" accidentally, and learned something about the analysis of jokes from my informant himself during my first fieldwork experience.

The person who delivered our heating oil was named John Vickery, a big, robust, grey-haired man about sixty years old. In negotiating the large hose from the truck to the oil tank, Mr. Vickery would often grumble about how he couldn't get around as easily as he used to. When he brought some oil to our house, I thought I'd practice my self-taught folklore collecting technique.

"Mr. Vickery, you don't know any jokes, do you?" I asked (Dorson said later that this wasn't a particularly effective fieldwork technique).

To my amazement, he said, "Yeah, I have a good joke I'll tell you. I like it because it's about an old man like me."

This old man was walking along the golf course, and there were three guys standing there ready to tee off, but the fourth had not shown up. So they asked the old man if he'd like to play a round with them. He said, "Well, sure; I've played a little golf." They said they played a fast game, but he said he'd give it a try. They said also that they played for money, but he said that was all right. So, they played nine holes and he beat them like a drum, won a lot of money. They played a second nine holes and he beat them again. Wanted to play a third round, but they said they wanted to go to the clubhouse and do some drinking. He said, "Okay," and so he proceeded to drink them under the table! One of them asked, "Look, old fellow, you beat us at golf, you took all our money, and drank us under the table. Doesn't old age have any disadvantages at all?" He thought for a minute and said, "Yeah, I can think of one. This morning when I woke up, I asked my wife to make love, and she said, 'What, after seven times last night?' You see, when you get old, your ***memory*** *begins to slip a bit!"*

Mr. Vickery enjoyed telling the joke because he identified closely with its protagonist, who isn't bothered in the least by old age and who in fact out-performs much younger men. In imagining the story, Mr. Vickery himself conquered time and youth, and achieved a moment's relief from his anxiety concerning the deterioration of his abilities.

Jokes can of course also function for groups as well as individuals. On a national level we have the cycle of jokes that accompany such disasters as the Atlanta murders, the attempted assassination of President Reagan, the accident at Three Mile Island, the deaths of Len Bias and Rock

Hudson, the near-death of Richard Pryor, the space shuttle explosion, and the accident at Chernobyl. Psychologists believe that these jokes relieve stress, serving "the same function . . . that jesters served in medieval times—providing comic relief in bad times." [1]

Other kinds of jokes serve as a kind of social cement, binding groups of people closer together. Sometimes these jokes are so esoteric, so group-bound, that they make no sense to at all outside the in-group. For example:

The famous folklorist Stith Thompson was giving a talk to a group of folklorists once, and he said, "X-1715.3," and the place erupted in laughter. Then he said, "X-1213.3"—explosions of laughter. Another fellow got up and said, "X-1213.1." Nothing. Then he said, "X-1718.1"—absolute silence. After the talk he asked, "What happened here?" He was told that some people can tell 'em and some can't.

To understand this joke one would have to know that Stith Thompson compiled the massive *Motif-Index of Folk Literature*[2] and that all numbers in the index beginning with X signal humorous stories. Folklorists would of course be acquainted with the basic narrative summaries designated by the numbers and would therefore need to hear only the numbers of the motifs to grasp Professor Thompson's meaning.

The statement "Whatever Lola wants, Stan Getz" would appeal primarily to those familiar with jazz, as would the question "Did you hear about the cow that drank some ink and 'Mood Indigo'?"

The folklorist Barre Toelken has in fact defined a folk group in terms of esoteric dynamics, writing that it is a "system of human interchange where the members of any group interrelate on a high context level of attitude, reference, connotation, sense of meaning, and customary behavior, precisely as members, and to be members, of that group." [3] But it was the University of Kentucky folklorist William Hugh Jansen who first called our attention to intragroup as well as intergroup elements in folklore in his 1959 article "The Esoteric-Exoteric Factor in Folklore."[4] Jansen wrote that the esoteric factor "frequently stems from the group sense of belonging and serves to defend and strengthen that sense . . . [and that it] arises from the special knowledge of a group and, intentionally or not, aids in preserving that knowledge." He gave as an example the response of a Kentucky mountain farmer who, when asked, "How are you?" replied, "Two to a hill." Jansen explained that farmers used to plant corn in hills, four seeds to the hill. "Thus two seedlings to a hill represents fifty per cent germination and his answer means a noncommittal 'So-so'—to the group which shares his esoteric knowledge." Esoteric factors in folklore, then, apply "to what one group thinks of itself and what it supposes others think of it."

Jansen went on to define the exoteric factor as "what one group thinks of another and what it thinks that other group thinks it thinks," pointing out that it is a "product of the same sense of belonging, for it may result from fear of, mystification about, or resentment of the group to which one does not belong." A fundamental illustration of the exoteric factor would be the cycle of "lightbulb" jokes that began years ago when the so-called "Polack jokes" were in oral tradition. These jokes now characterize such diverse groups as bluegrass musicians, psychiatrists, surrealists, and feminists:

How many Polacks does it take to screw in a lightbulb? Four. One to hold the bulb and three to turn the ladder.

How many bluegrass musicians . . . ? Four. One to screw it in and three to complain about its being electric.

How many psychiatrists . . .? Only one but the bulb has to really want to be changed.

How many surrealists . . . ? A fish.

How many feminists . . .? That's ***not*** funny.

Members of religious groups can express criticism of other religions through jokes. I grew up in western Kentucky as a Southern Baptist and can remember clearly being warned about the strange ways of Catholics. This joke corresponds to that attitude:

Two guys were in an airplane and the plane developed engine trouble, and it was clear that they were going to be killed. One said to the other, "Well, this is it. We are going to die. Are you religious?" The other one said, "No, are you?" The first one said, "No. I'm not either, but we ought to do something religious because we're going to be dead in a few seconds. Don't you remember anything religious that we could do?" The other guy said, "Well, I used to live next door to a Catholic church, and I used to hear those people in there. Maybe I could quote some of it." "We only have about twenty seconds left," said the other guy, "so go ahead." The guy said, "Under the B, 7; under the I, 5; under the N, 21 . . . ."

Yankees tell jokes about Southerners, Republicans about Democrats, and citizens from one state tell jokes about other states, which sometimes leads to hard feelings. For example, North Dakotans became so angry at the jokes Montanans told about them that they decided to march to Washington to protest. When last heard from, they were more than halfway to Seattle.[5]

And colleges poke fun at other colleges. According to the students at the University of North Carolina, they don't teach driver's ed at North Carolina State anymore because the tractor broke down.[6] Another "culture versus agriculture" joke is that State's idea of a wine and cheese party is watching Hee Haw with Velveeta and Ripple.[7]

But of course the most common type of exoteric joke is the "ethnic" joke, which pokes fun at the stereotypical characteristics of Poles, Italians, Mexicans, Jews, Blacks, Scandinavians, the Irish, even mainstream WASPS—the kind of jokes responsible for the success of such comedians as Don Rickles and Jackie Vernon. Folks in the urban North tell many jokes about Appalachian people. Here is an example of one that illustrates how a story may contain both esoteric and exoteric qualities, depending on the context in which it is told:

A guy died and went to heaven. St. Peter was showing him around, and the guy thought it was wonderful. It was great—a beautiful place, just paradise. They went around the corner, and there was a bunch of people in chains, and the guy asked St. Peter why in the world these people were chained. St. Peter replied, "That's a bunch of hillbillies, and every Friday at 5:00 p.m., they want to head home for the weekend!" [8]

I first heard this story in Columbus, Ohio, told in such a manner as to express ridicule of Appalachian migrants in the city who feel compelled to return home every weekend. The story mirrors the sentiments expressed in the riddle-joke "What are the three R's hillbillies learn in grade school?" Answer: "Readin', 'Ritin', and Route 23 (or Road to Dayton)." But I also heard the joke told by Mary Lozier, an Appalachian woman who felt that it conveyed the idea that to Appalachian people, eastern Kentucky was infinitely more paradisiacal than Heaven itself.

Mary Lozier lives near South Portsmouth, Kentucky, a few miles northwest of the northern boundary of the Big Sandy Valley region, which extends, roughly, from Ashland to Elkhorn City, along the tributaries of the Levisa and Tug Forks of the Big Sandy River. I conducted fieldwork "up Sandy" during the early 1970s, collecting beliefs, legends, ballads, and some forty humorous narratives.[9] These humorous stories, all on the esoteric side of the continuum, are "true" local character anecdotes rather than fictional jokes, with the exception of five tall tales, which are nevertheless associated with specific persons. Each story centers around the comic discomfiture of mildly to considerably "deviant" Big Sandians, with half of the stories involving deception in the form of either pranks or lies.

In a general category of discomfiture stories those discomfited include a couple of travelers, an adolescent who is laughed at when his voice changes in the middle of a sentence, a Black man, and a man with a huge nose. In the latter story, the teller admires the clever retort of a big-nosed man who's insulted by a waitress:

There were a lot of people staying at this place and one of them had one of the biggest, highest noses you ever saw. It was an awful big, long nose. He was a big bony-faced fellow, I guess six and a half feet high—a big man. Well, the waitress came around and saw his nose and couldn't help asking how come his nose was so big. But he was hard to get ahead of. He said, "Madam, I kept it out of other people's business until it got its growth."[10]

One of the travelers who is discomfited is a man named Darvey from Pikeville who is forced to spend the night with some folks "up in the mountains":

Mr. Darvey got up in the mountains about 9:00 that night and he couldn't get back home, so he had to spend the night with a farmer. He went to bed, and just every once in a while his bed seemed to wiggle around a lot, so he lay there until about midnight, and then he hollered for the farmer to come in there, said there was something wrong with his bed. The farmer said it was just his old hog under the bed. It would come in every night and sleep under the bed.[11]

Three stories involve the discomfiture of animals. In two of these narratives, hogs, chickens, and geese somehow get into moonshine whiskey and become drunk and befuddled. The third is about the chaos that ensues when a dog becomes entangled with a kettle of hot dumplings:

There was a man had a work day going on. It was common to have work days for timbering and rafting logs. There were twenty or thirty men there and a big kettle of dumplings, a big kettle with a bail on it. They were eating when they heard a commotion outside, and they went out to see what was going on, leaving the bail up on the kettle of hot dumplings. When they went out, the old hound dog came a-running into the house and ran his nose down into that kettle of dumplings, and when he jerked his head up to run back out, he got the bail caught behind his ears, so he went out the door and into the woods, with the dumplings, just like he was chasing a fox![12]

A social event like this one being upset by a raucous, hell's-a-poppin' disturbance is of course reminiscent of many of the Sut Lovingood yarns, "Sicily Burns's Wedding" in particular. Four of these stories included whiskey drinkers who were discomfited, and the next story combines two types of victims of discomfiture—drunks and those easily frightened:

A man accused of being a witch invited this man, who was pretty drunk, and his two brothers to supper. He made the table jump and bounce around, and then the door flew open and a black cat came in and walked around and made all kinds of a scratching racket, and just scared those boys to death! They jumped up and ran, and the one who was drunk lost his false teeth in a manure pile! Next morning his sister went out and found his false teeth in the manure pile.[13]

Another body of discomfiture humor in the Big Sandy area is pointed toward the numbskulls: a man chops off a limb on which he is sitting; another thinks that macaroni is grubworms; another, unfamiliar with ice cream, spreads it on bread and eats it. Two young boys who've never seen a train are frightened by one; two more get in trouble with authorities in Ashland when they tell them that they're from Lovely and Beauty, two small towns up Sandy; and one young man believes that a parrot in Catlettsburg speaks to

him in a familiar way. The last story in this category turns on a man's ignorance of a certain word:

This man was going with a girl and was wanting to marry her, but she wouldn't even consider it. He kept on insisting that they get married until she finally told him, "Why Sid, I'm a hermaphrodite." "Ah," he said, "that's all right, honey. I'll go to your church and you can go to mine. I'm a Campbellite."[14]

All the other stories I collected involve discomfiture brought about by deception, with those discomfited including drummers, children, the elderly, braggers, numbskulls, tricksters, law enforcement authorities, and the stingy. A man named Tackett lied so frequently that he acquired the name "Lyin' Frank":

These kids were gathering up and eating paw-paws, when Old Man Lyin' Frank came along, and they begged him to tell them a story. But he said, "No, I can't do it. Don't have time." "Why not?" they asked. "Well, kids, your mother is dying, and I'm heading over to Mud Creek to fetch a doctor for her." Those kids threw those paw-paws every which way and ran a-screaming and crying over the hill. When they got within hearing of their mother, she came running to meet them thinking that a snake had bit one of them the way they were crying and screaming. They said, "Momma, Old Man Frank Tackett said you was a-dyin'." She said, "That old devil! I was just dyeing yarn."[15]

Frank Tackett's reputation as a liar became so widespread that folks sought him out to compete with him:

Lyin' Frank Tackett met a drummer [salesman] up on the mountain and the drummer says, "Sir, do you know Frank Tackett?" He says, "I don't know whether I do or not. What do you want with him?" "Well, sir, they tell me than he is the biggest liar in the mountains of Kentucky, and I've got a bigger one to tell than he has." Lyin' Frank says, "For heaven's sake, mister, tell me, so if you don't see him I can tell him." "Well," the drummer says, "my father cleared an acre of ground for a turnip patch, and he put a ten-rail fence around it and sowed it down to turnips. One seed came up in that patch, and it grew and grew so big that it pushed that fence down around that acre of ground." "Boy," he says, "that's a dandy. I don't see how he can beat that." Frank says, "I've got to go." The drummer asks, "Where are you going?" He says, "We're building a kettle over here so big that you can be on one side and me on the other, and I can hit it with a ten-pound sledge hammer and you can't hear it ring." The drummer asks, "Why would you want a kettle that big for?" "To cook that turnip in," he says.[16]

That story is of course a tall tale. Other tall tales up Sandy involve unbelievably strong men, remarkable fishermen, and men who live to an extraordinarily old age.

Those familiar with the body of literature known as "Old Southwestern humor" will recognize in these oral narratives most of the characteristics of that genre: deception, vernacular speech, exaggerated tall talk, indelicacy, raciness, cruelty, violence, discomfiture, comic portraiture, exuberant vitality, and story-telling itself, tall tales and character anecdotes in particular. Clearly, frontier humor is valued up Sandy. In fact, the Big Sandy collective persona, the pervasive regional "character" in these stories, is much akin to Sut Lovingood, the protagonist of George Washington Harris's writing, which is generally considered to be the jewel in the crown of Old Southwestern Humor. What scholars have said about Sut and his peers can lead us to an understanding of what these stories may mean to Big Sandians.

James Penrod, for example, has written that the "pranksters of the Southwestern yarns were motivated by a natural delight in physical discomfort or upset dignity, by native prejudices, or by the desire for revenge on a person or group . . . [and they] particularly delighted in victimizing pompous, hypocritical, literal-minded, and superstitious people of any age, class, or race."[17] Arlin Turner maintains that the "yarns which Sut tells . . . have rarely been equaled

for the abundance of sheer physical pain . . ., for the embarrassing exposure of man and woman from uncomplimentary angles, physically and otherwise." [18] M. Thomas Inge points out that Sut's pranks result in "rough justice," because nearly all of his victims are either "hypocritical, falsely self-righteous, sinful, or downright criminal." [19] Inge goes on to say that Sut is candid and honest, opposes what he doesn't like, understands himself well, makes the best out of life as it is, and "typifies the good and the bad in the customs and character of the backwoodsman and mountaineer." [20] Both Sut and the Big Sandy storyteller lash out at and expose pretension, smugness, hypocrisy, and other forms of non-conformity to group norms. They punish their victims by discomfiting them through deception and trickery. As the folklorist Pat Mullen puts it, local character anecdotes "are part of the oral tradition of a community and reveal more about society's reaction to deviance than about the deviant . . . [and that when deviants] "break a norm, they are making the norm evident to the community, and the stories about this violation serve as outgoing reminders of the norm." [21] Thus, when Big Sandians poke fun at those who are uninformed, stingy, immature, boastful, witless, drunk, or too easily frightened, they are embracing the values of an inverse identity: generosity, maturity, moderation, cleverness, wisdom, sobriety, and courage.

The Big Sandy storyteller also reminds one of the character Jack of the "Jack Tales." Tom Davis sees Jack as a clever but ordinary man who uses his own good wits and the common artifacts of his culture to defeat the forces of chaos and to secure justice and prosperity for himself and his fellows in a world that is capricious and amoral.[22] Similarly,

Gurney Norman believes that Jack's "native energy, wit and ingenuity" are qualities that define courage and persistence and that he is "representative of the common people he lived among and who produced him in that, above all, he is never a quitter."[23] Seen from this perspective, local character anecdotes up Sandy are, both structurally and thematically, modern versions of Jack tales.

Many of the characteristics outlined in the discussion of esoteric Big Sandy humorous narratives appear in the exoteric stories of the adjacent counties of Harlan and Letcher. Leonard Roberts includes several stories that belittle an out-group—Irishmen, or "Arshmen"—in his book *Sang Branch Settlers.*[24] Almost all of these stories contain the pattern of the discomfiture of deviants through deception. The Arshmen Pat and Mike are presented in the stories as being absolute fools who don't understand the Appalachian experience. Their failure to understand Appalachian speech; their lack of knowledge of such things as ticks, tumblebugs, pepper, guns, and cushaws; and all-around ignorance result in their extreme discomfiture. Common sense and native wit, including, of course, the ability to deceive, are valued highly in these stories. Here is an example:

Mike went along the road till he run into another old Arshman and they decided to stay together. They was allas hungry and trying to get enough to eat some way. They come to a gyarden with a lot of red pepper in it. They didn't know what it was, of course, but they was hungry enough to try to get 'em a bait of it. Mike said, "Sam, you go up there and watch for the mon and I'll climb through in and get us some of that nice red fruit." Sam watched and Mike jumped in the gyarden and got him a few pods of that red pepper, poked one or two pods in his mouth. Come on out with water running outten his eyes, like he was crying. The other'n said, "Well, what are you crying about?" He said, "I'm crying because my pore old granny didn't get none of this good fruit before she died." Well, Sam took a pod and poked it in his mouth. Chawed a-while, tears come to his eyes. He said, "Well, fat o' my Christ, if your old granny liked this stuff she orght to a been dead forty year ago."[25]

Another form of outsider about whom exoteric folklore exists in Appalachia is the tourist/summer resident, especially in the mountains of North Carolina. The local attitude toward these interlopers is expressed succinctly in this piece from the *Watauga Democrat* in early 1983:

FRANKLIN (AP)—During the past 10 to 15 years, newcomers have been buying up the North Carolina Appalachians to retire or build vacation homes, but some longtime mountain folk say they don't like it. . . .

"I wouldn't sell an inch of land to them," said Ollie Mae, 59, of the Cowee community in Macon County. "I love my dogs, cats, and chickens. When outsiders get in, they tell you to get rid of them.

"We have some real nice Florida neighbors," she said. "But when my husband said he'd like to get a pig and raise one more country ham, they said, 'Don't get a pig. We'll smell it.'"

"The way I see it, about the only thing we cultivate anymore is Floridians," said [Cloyd] Bolick, a rural mail carrier and semiretired farmer.[26]

A growing body of exoteric folklore is beginning to emerge that expresses this attitude. For example, the folk call all tourists "tourons," a play, of course, on "morons," and people from Florida "Florons." Tourons and Florons are ridiculed because they, like Pat and Mike, are ignorant of mountain ways.

Jim Wayne Miller tells, for example, about tourons who saw a pile of discarded milk cartons and thought it was a "cow's nest." Many of these outsiders are wealthy and drive huge cars, but are inept when it comes to driving in the mountains. Some jokes center around lost tourists and their rude manner of asking questions:

Willard Watson is Doc Watson's cousin. A lot of people come down Wildcat Road and bother Willard, and they ask him, "Where's this road go?" Willard says, "Why, children, I've lived here all my life, and I've never seen it go anywhere!"

The funniest one I've ever heard is about a guy sitting by the side of the road and a lost tourist drives up and asks rather rudely, "How do you get to Boone?" The old man says, "Well, sometimes I walk, and sometimes my son-in-law takes me in his pickup truck."

So, by lying to tourists, by putting them on, deceiving them, and responding to their rudeness with clever retorts, folks in North Carolina's "high country" assume, once again, the role of trickster, who restores social order and balance from the chaos brought about by people who deviate from their norms. Sometime they best the outsider by understatement:

A fellow was driving his mule and wagon down the road, and a touron came flying by in his car and ran into the mule, hurt it badly. He got out and said, "Gosh, did I hurt your mule?" The farmer said, "Well, if you think you done him any good, I'd be happy to pay you fer it."

And sometimes they emerge victorious by being crafty:

A farmer pulled his hay wagon out into the Blowing Rock road in front of a tourist who came tearing down the road not looking where he was going. He hit the wagon and did a lot of damage to his car. He jumped out hot under the collar, all jacked out of shape, and said, "Look what you've done to my car!" The farmer said, "Well, I'm sorry. I know it was my fault, but the law will be along in a few minutes, so just sit back and cool off. Don't get nervous or you'll bust a gut. Here, have a drink of liquor while we wait." So the guy decided to have a drink, and began to cool off with every swallow he'd take, and by the time the law got there, the farmer said, "Why, this S.O.B. was drunk, and he ran right into me!"

Just as John Vickery experienced triumph over the young golfers through his joke, Appalachian folks are healed through their exoteric humorous narratives. As Barre Toelken puts it, humor "often functions in such a way as to allow a joke teller to bring up a topic of some anxiety among members of a group and then to demonstrate or experience superiority over the implied threat by reducing it to something laughable.'' [27] Moreover, these storytellers are still like Sut and Jack, surviving and prevailing through native wit and intelligence, relying upon what Gurney Norman calls ''the latent power of native tradition, power that, upon rediscovery, may be released as a spiritual impulse and find expression in a healthy politics.'' Such power may help all Appalachian people, like Jack, to manage to ''land on [their] feet in triumph.'' [28]

Notes

[1]UCLA psychologist Jacqueline Goodchilds in ''At the Gallows: Black Humor Cuts the Stress From Disasters Down to Size, Psychologists Say,'' *Winston-Salem Journal,* 25 May 1986, sec. A, p. 2. For a perceptive analysis of disaster jokes by a folklorist as well as a bibliography of recent folkloristic interpretations of the humor of disaster, see Elliott Oring, ''Jokes and the Discourse on Disaster,'' *Journal of American Folklore* 100 (1987): 276–86.

[2]Stith Thompson, *Motif-Index of Folk Literature* (Bloomington: Indiana University Press, 1955).

[3]Barre Toelken, *The Dynamics of Folklore* (Boston: Houghton Mifflin, 1979), p. 52.

[4]William Hugh Jansen, ''The Esoteric-Exoteric Factor in Folklore,'' in *The Study of Folklore,* ed. Alan Dundes (Englewood Cliffs, N.J.: Prentice-Hall, 1965), pp. 43–51.

[5]William E. Schmidt, ''Poking Fun is Statewide Pastime,'' *Winston-Salem Journal,* 1 Nov. 1981, sec. E, p. 14.

[6]Cherin Poovey, ''The Joke's On State,'' *Winston-Salem*

Journal, 11 Dec. 1981, sec. D, p. 27.

[7]Ibid.

[8]For a good discussion of migrant jokes, see Clyde B. McCoy and Virginia McCoy Watkins, "Stereotypes of Appalachian Migrants," in *The Invisible Minority: Urban Appalachians,* ed. William W. Philliber and Clyde McCoy, with Harry C. Dillingham (Lexington: The University Press of Kentucky, 1981), pp. 20–31.

[9]For a fuller description of the Big Sandy Valley region as well as discussions of folklore up Sandy, see William E. Lightfoot, *Folklore of the Big Sandy Valley of Eastern Kentucky* (Ph.D. diss., Indiana University, 1976).

[10]Told by Henry Matney. Motifs X130, "Other physical disabilities"; X137, "Humor of ugliness"; and J1300, "Officiousness or foolish question rebuked." This and the following narratives have been referenced to Ernest Baughman's *Type and Motif Index of England and North America* (The Hague, The Netherlands: Mouton and Company, 1966).

[11]Told by Virgie Justice.

[12]Told by Harvey Rhodes.

[13]Told by Ruth Lowe.

[14]Told by Curtis Barber. Type 16988G, "Misunderstood words lead to comic results"; and Motif J1738, "Ignorance of religious matters."

[15]Told by Hassel Tackett. Type 1920B, "The one says, 'I have no time to lie' and yet lies."

[16]Told by Hassel Tackett. Types 1920A, "The first tells of the great cabbage . . . the other of the great kettle to cook it in"; 1960D, "The great vegetable"; 1960F, "The great kettle"; and Motif X14312.1, "Lies about big turnips."

[17]James H. Penrod, "The Folk Hero As Prankster in the Old Southwestern Yarns," *Kentucky Folklore Record* 11 (1956): 6.

[18]Arlin Turner, "Seeds of the Literary Revolt in the Humor of the Old Southwest," *Louisiana Historical Quarterly* 39 (1956): 150.

[19]M. Thomas Inge, "Sut Lovingood: An Examination of the Nature of a 'Nat'ral Born Durn'd Fool,'" *Tennessee*

Historical Quarterly 19 (1960): 245.

[20]Ibid., p. 251.

[21]Patrick B. Mullen, *I Heard the Old Fishermen Say: Folklore of the Texas Gulf Coast* (Austin: University of Texas Press, 1978), p. 116, 121.

[22]Charles Thomas Davis, III, "The Changing World of the Jack Tales," *Tennessee Folklore Bulletin* 45 (1979): 96-106. Also see the "Jack Tale" issue of the *North Carolina Folklore Journal* 26 (1978).

[23]Gurney Norman, notes to the June Appal recording *Ancient Creek* (June Appal O11, 1976) pp. 3–4.

[24]Leonard Roberts, *Sang Branch Settlers: Folksongs and Tales of a Kentucky Mountain Family* (Austin: University of Texas Press, 1974), p. 245.

[25]Ibid., p. 245.

[26]*The Watauga* [N.C.] *Democrat*, 28 March 1983, sec. A, p. 2.

[27]Toelken, p. 268.

[28]Norman, p. 4.

''The Devil Made Me Do It'' versus ''God Told Me''

BILLY EDD WHEELER

I have one thing in common with Abraham Lincoln. When I was growing up I liked to imitate preachers, especially the hellfire-and-damnation kind. Abe did that too, as a teenager, my research tells me. It also tells me that Abe was better at it than I was. As a boy he had the uncanny ability to recount sermons word for word, gesture for gesture, and his favorite preachers were the ones who waved their arms about ''like they were fighting bees.''

I don't know if Abe ever got in trouble over it, but I bet he did. You know how folks are about religion. You start imitating their preachers and you're apt to get in trouble. Even if you do it as a scholar, as the late Dr. Cratis Williams found out, you might get called on the carpet, because someone in the audience will think you're making fun of a preacher they know. (This happened to Dr. Williams once or twice, even though he had great sympathy and love for Appalachian people, and intended no disrespect.)

Granddaddy Wheeler didn't think much of Presbyterians.

''They won't worsh feet, nor nothing,'' he would say. ''And the preachers write down what they're going to say before they get to the church!'' He thought that was the height of insincerity and high-uppityness. ''Why, they even figure out what songs they're gonna sing, too, beforehand.''

''How does your preacher do it, Daddy?'' I asked him once, on the way to a holy-roller service near Montcoal, West Virginia, when I was home from college (a Presbyterian school, by the way, Warren Wilson College, located in western North Carolina).

''He preaches from the heart,'' Granddad replied.

''How far did he go in school?''

''He don't need schoolin','' he said sternly, absolutely. ''The Lord puts the words in his mouth.''

That night I got a good dose of spontaneous fundamentalist preaching. It was spirited, all right, but it left me thinking that God must have a limited vocabulary. The preacher was one of those shouters who couldn't have used more than one hundred words in his entire sermon that went on for an hour, and he ended most of his phrases with a grunting, cough-like ''uh!'' Sometimes the ''uh!'' came after every word, depending upon how worked up the preacher was, sort of like spiritual hiccups.

It is a fascinating, almost hypnotizing pattern of speech these preachers use. Here is a sample of it, as nearly word for word as I can recall it:

''Now, friends and neighbors, Paul was called—called by God—to walk down that dusty road to the Sea of Galilee—uh! Was he alone-uh? No-uh! He had Silas with him. Thank God, brothers and sisters, he didn't have to walk that long, hot, dusty road by hisself. No-uh! He had Silas-uh—with him-uh! And who did Silas have? Was Silas alone by hisself-uh? No, thank God, he had Paul-uh!—with him-uh!—and Paul he had Silas-uh! Praise God, they was to-geth-er-uh! Together-uh! Paul and Silas and Silas and Paul-uh! Not Paul-uh!—and not Silas-uh!—but Paul *and* Silas-uh! One time-uh, Paul-uh, stubbed his toe-uh, and Silas-uh, was right there-uh to catch him before he fell-uh, on his face in that hot dusty, that long, hot, dusty road that led-uh, to Galilee-uh!"

After the sermon there was a foot-washing. This can be a touching ceremony, people humbling themselves, crying as they wash each other's feet, testifying, praising God. It also looked refreshing, as it was a hot July night and the church was not air-conditioned, but I didn't participate. (Too self-conscious and Presbyterian, don't you know. Besides, I hadn't changed socks in two days and I had tennis shoes on. Anybody bent over my bare feet could easily have gotten a terminal case of pinkeye.)

When the foot-washing and the singing and praying were over and folks were hugging each other goodbye, my grandfather introduced me to the preacher on the way out.

"I was fascinated by your sermon, Preacher," I said.

He looked at me as he wiped his sweaty brow with a handkerchief, extending his hand, smiling, but trying to size me up, too, I had no doubt. For after all I hadn't complimented him exactly, as everyone else had, and he knew I was a college boy. He was in his mid-twenties, I guessed, not much older than I was at the time, and his grip was strong. He probably worked in the coal mines or did logging work to have such a calloused hand.

"Could I ask you a question?" I said. He nodded.

"Where did you find that part in the Bible about Paul stubbing his toe?"

"It ain't in the Bible," he replied, still smiling.

"Then how do you know it happened?" I asked, as humbly as I could.

"God told me," he said. And that was that.

On the way home Granddaddy Wheeler and his second

wife, Gussie, went over the high points of the service, declaring that it was a doozy and that the preacher was in extra good form. "And you may not believe it, Billy," Granddaddy said, "but he didn't even finish high school."

"I believe it, Daddy," I said.

Lest you, dear Reader, think that I write this little essay from a vantage point of assumed superiority, I hasten to correct you. I admit the illiterate preacher is not *my* cup of tea, but he reaches some people that my favorite preacher, Fred Ohler, for example, could not touch. People who are not necessarily dense or illiterate themselves. People who like their religion strong and simple and uncomplicated, who don't care about enlightened and philosophical sermons that subtly argue the fine points of living the Christian life, balancing between sin and salvation, God and the Devil.

These fire-and-brimstone preachers scared the holy dickens out of me when I was growing up. I thought the Devil must be a mighty powerful man to lurk in so many dark corners (like the Boogeyman) and to cover so much territory and influence in daily living—down to lipstick, the length of skirts, smoking, drinking, sex (even thinking about it), hair too short or too long, working on Sunday, playing cards or shooting pool and almost any form of having fun.

No matter how much preachers put him down, I used to want to throw in with the Devil, take a chance and have some fun. But I didn't have the nerve. Philosophy and religion courses in college helped a little and I began to give up thinking of the Devil as a person, and I began to experiment with dipping my toes into the Lake of Enlightenment and Free Thinking and Semi-Free Living, though I never got ready to make the whole plunge. I could buy into sin on the installment plan but never go whole hog and make an outright purchase. I stopped worrying about the Devil the longer I stayed in college, away from fundamentalist preachers—though he still lurks in some of the beer halls and dark hollows of my mind.

Today fundamentalist preaching is big business. On TV, at least. Oh, the preachers are well dressed and groomed and their message is a little more sophisticated, sometimes, but not always, and they still reach a segment of society that believes the Devil is a real being and is alive and well, not just in Appalachia but in "mainstream" America as well. (You don't have to be a hillbilly to fall for their pitches.) And sometimes when these preachers decide to run for political office, or have to justify some outlandish statement or action or explain how they arrived at certain conclusions, they invoke the same proclamation that that preacher did in Montcoal, West Virginia, which is the birthright of fundamentalist preachers: *God told me.*

Often when I go too far and indulge in something that I think is sinful, like watching something I shouldn't be watching in the movies or on video (TV preachers watch the real thing!), I invoke the phrase which is the counterpart of the one used by preachers and is the birthright of us everyday mortals: *The Devil made me do it!*

Granddaddy Wheeler was a little more honest about it when he lost control, or at least he explained it a different way. Some years before he died he was having an argument with his son-in-law, Claude Jarrell, a little banty-rooster of a guy who sometimes drank too much and was prone to fight and who was always in the process of separating or getting back together with my Aunt Jean. Claude had been told by Sheriff Johnny Protan not to come up on the hill and bother Jean, but there he was, at the gate of Granddaddy Wheeler's house in Sylvester, with a knife in his hand trimming his nails and waving it at Granddad now and again, saying, "You ain't long for this world, old man."

Granddaddy Wheeler was normally a peaceable man, but he didn't take kindly to threats, especially from Claude. He

got red in the face as he told me about it, referring to Claude as that *thang,* not wanting to dignify him by calling him by name. He said, "Billy, I reckon the Lord left me for a minute. If that thang had-a come into this house—just took one step in it—I'd-a salvated his jaw and kicked him right square-up in the crack of his britches. I know it's a awful thing to say, but I'd-a done it."

Granddaddy said the Lord left him. I say the Devil made me do it. But I'm not sure I believe it, and I'm not sure it gets me off the hook. I still can't dive whole hog into that lake and get wet all over. And I don't think I could enjoy it if I could, which proves, partly at least, that you can't get above your raising. Sometimes in my mind I am still a child of Appalachia sitting in a one-room church, mesmerized by a preacher with fire in his eyes pointing his bony finger at me, reminding me that the Devil is everywhere, all the time, watching me, waiting for me to step over the line. And I remember the faith of Granddaddy Wheeler who died at age ninety-six, confident that he'd beaten the Devil, certain that a better home awaited him on the other side. Granddaddy Wheeler couldn't *wait* to die. He longed for it. Tears would streak down his cheeks as he rocked in his old rocking chair and sang, "There's a better home a-waiting . . . in the sky, Lord, in the sky."

And I'm not sure I believe that, either, that heaven is a real place with golden streets and all. But Granddad did and because of it he died happy. As several people have said, "If it helps get you through the night, don't knock it."

Abe Lincoln read the Bible as a boy, along with all the great books available in his day, and grew up in a strict, moralistic society in the wilderness of southern Indiana. Once when he was asked how he felt about religion he replied, in words to this effect, "If what I do seems right, then it must be good, and if it seems wrong, then it must be bad . . . and that's about as far as I've got with it."

One thing I *don't* have in common with Abe is that he was a model kid and I wasn't. Abe probably never had to say, "The Devil made me do it." Of course, he didn't have to run the gamut of temptation that faced us twentieth-century kids (though I imagine the Devil was pretty busy in Abe's day, too), even us older ones, and especially the young ones of today, what with X-rated everything available everywhere in living color.

An old adage has it that the Devil can't stand the sound of laughter, that he slinks away from it. Well, then, seems to me, the way to beat the Devil is to laugh a lot and have a lot of fun. Seems to me that God, if He's worth His salt at all, ought to be everywhere, just like the Devil, not just in the church house. He ought to be in our workplaces and at the ballpark, on camping trips and at yard sales, in our lovemaking and in our fighting, in hospitals, pool halls, music, sadness, joy, good times, bad times, singing, sorrowing.

Shucks, I guess He ought to be with us even when we're sinning . . . like watching an X-rated movie—oops!, I didn't mean to say that. I don't watch those things. I—uh, well, I *did* watch one one time, but I didn't really enjoy it . . . not all of it, anyhow, and besides I only did it for educational purposes. Really. Fact, I don't know *why* I did it. Yeah, I do: The Devil made me do it!

Blame it on the Devil, that's the ticket.

Well, there's one good thing you can say about the Devil, and you've got to admit you admire him for it: he's always on the job!

AUGUST HOUSE PUBLISHERS

OF RELATED INTEREST:

Dreaming in Color
19 Stories by Ruth Moose
Hardcover, $15.95
Clyde Edgerton: "Ruth Moose writes wonderfully wise and funny stories about people we know."

The Wreath Ribbon Quilt
Stories by Ruth Moose
Trade paperback, $8.95
Lee Smith: "By turns touching, raucous and wise."

Jujitsu for Christ
A Novel by Jack Butler
Hardback, $14.95
New York Times Book Review: "Brilliant and telling . . . sums up the whole strange world of the post-segregation South, a place simmering with previously undreamed-of possibilities."

The Errand of the Eye
A Novel by Hope Norman Coulter
Hardback, $15.95
Southern Magazine: "Beautifully written, powerful . . . keenly observed."

Laughter in Appalachia
Appalachian Mountain Humor
Loyal Jones and Billy Edd Wheeler, Editors
Southern Living: "A delightful, giggle-a-minute collection of yarns told simply and eloquently by mountain folks for whom humor is a way of life."

Mexican-American Folklore
Legends, Songs, Festivals, Crafts & Proverbs
Edited by John O. West
Winner of the Border Regional Library Association "Best Book" Award for 1988.

Civil War Women
Trade Paperback, $8.95 (fiction)
Publishers Weekly: "Elegant or restrained, proud or self-deprecating, the voices in this collection resound."

AUGUST HOUSE, INC., PUBLISHERS
PO Box 3223, Little Rock, AR 72203
1-800-527-0924